BY TERRY MCMILLAN

It Was the Way She Said It

It's Not All Downhill from Here

I Almost Forgot About You

Who Asked You?

Getting to Happy

The Interruption of Everything

A Day Late and a Dollar Short

How Stella Got Her Groove Back

Waiting to Exhale

Breaking Ice: An Anthology of Contemporary African-American Fiction (ed.)

Disappearing Acts

Mama

IT WAS
THE WAY
SHE SAID IT

IT WAS THE WAY SHE SAID IT

Short Stories, Essays, and Wisdom

TERRY MCMILLAN

Edited by Kristine Bell

Foreword by Ishmael Reed

BALLANTINE BOOKS

NEW YORK

Ballantine Books
An imprint of Random House
A division of Penguin Random House LLC
1745 Broadway, New York, NY 10019
randomhousebooks.com
penguinrandomhouse.com

Permission and source credits are located on page 223.

Hardcover ISBN 9780593357149
Ebook ISBN 9780593357156

Printed in the United States of America on acid-free paper

1st Printing

FIRST EDITION

BOOK TEAM: Production editor: Loren Noveck • Managing editor: Pam Alders •
Production manager: Katie Zilberman • Copy editor: Aja Pollock •
Proofreaders: Julie Ehlers, Taylor McGowan, and Katie Powers

Interior art: frenta/Adobe Stock

Book design by Ralph Fowler

The authorized representative in the EU for product safety and
compliance is Penguin Random House Ireland, Morrison Chambers,
32 Nassau Street, Dublin D02 YH68, Ireland. https://eu-contact.penguin.ie.

Dedicated to Virginia Dunwell

CONTENTS

Terry McMillan, the People's Choice

Ishmael Reed

When I began teaching at Berkeley, I didn't view writing classes as a basket-weaving exercise—as the right has stereotyped them—but as a place where I might discover new talent.

I found that some of the students wrote as well as any published writer. When I included student writers in my anthology *From Totems to Hip-Hop,* I found that teachers assembled at the National Council of Teachers of English couldn't distinguish between the student pieces and those that canonized authors had written.

Terry spoke about our writing class in her 1999 commencement speech at UC Berkeley, which is included in this volume. In that speech, Terry recalled how I "told [her she] could write" but dismissed my compliment as "bogus." I did more than compliment her, I published her.

In 1972, Al Young and I had published the first *Yardbird Reader* with artist Glenn Myles and sculptor Doyle Foreman. Terry, a literary rookie at that time, was published in *Yardbird Reader* volume 5, to which she contributed "The End," one of the stories that appears in this collection. Her story stood alongside those of some lauded writers who appeared in the same issue. She belonged there. Mona Simpson, who was in the same class as Terry, was also included; Mona is the former publisher of *The Paris Review.*

At Berkeley, Terry was effervescent. Bubbling over with energy. Hip. Little did I know that she would shake up the world of Black literature.

I kept in contact with Terry after she graduated. I even helped her get a job at the University of Wyoming, Laramie. John Wideman and I visited the school, and the English department chair asked me to recommend someone. Terry it was.

A little-known fact about Terry is that she appeared as an actor in the now-classic *Personal Problems* project, which first aired on the late Steve Cannon's WBAI radio show. The film version, which the late Bill Gunn directed in 1980, and which starred Vertamae Grosvenor, was hailed by *New York* magazine as one of the best films ever shot in New York.

We made the *Personal Problems* film for $40,000. It was shown at the National Gallery of Art in Washington in 2019 and is streamed by the Criterion Collection. The tapes of Terry as an actor are stored in my archives at the University of Delaware. They show that she could have succeeded in Hollywood if she'd desired.

One day, Terry called and asked whether she should go beyond the publisher and promote her books herself. I told her that she should have her publisher promote the books. She didn't take my advice. She traveled to church groups and bookstores, where she promoted her work. As for her most famous novel, *Waiting to Exhale,* she was one of three Black women who made the *New York Times* bestseller list in 1992. The other two excellent writers had powerful sponsors, which is the traditional way that a Black writer becomes a divo or diva. This "one-at-a-time" mentality is still the case.

Those other two bestselling authors were awarded Pulitzers, an award denied to Terry, who wrote just as well. Never mind; Terry was the people's choice. Why?

The characters delineated by McMillan are the ones with whom millions of Black people are familiar, whether they be upscale or older adults living on social security and maybe hiding some outside income. All the themes of the blues are expressed in her work: economic insecurity, betrayal, and the conflicts between men and women. Yes, American men can be a mess. I've been there. However, many contemporary portrayals of Black men have given rise to the Black Bogeyman genre, a multimillion-dollar product that critic C. Liegh McInnis says "sells better than sex." Even Harvey Weinstein has made some money from a Black Bogeyman product.

Terry's Black men are not one-dimensional brutes or "soulless monsters" whose aim is to torment women. They are complex, multifaceted individuals, as shown in this passage from "The End."

> Every dull ass morning I drive the same dull ass way, wear the same dull ass uniform, and feel the same dull ass way going to this lousy job. And look at that old bitch over there. Got enough hairspray in her hair to starch a laundry of clothes. She can afford to bleach her hair to lightening frightening blond and tease it so everybody can see it cause she's rich. In her Mercedes-Benz, bitch. All them honkies is rich, including the women. This must be her neighbor behind her. Seems like rich people don't mind tailgating each other. But if it was me behind em, they'd

change lanes. I'd like to run into one of em and get me some insurance, something ugly. I bet that dude is in Ford's office from eight to five, and I bet he has clean fingernails, and I bet he loves his job. I bet he doesn't mind getting up in the morning. He can drink coffee and eat doughnuts all day and have lunch with the fellas. Probably drinks wine with his lunch and eats his steaks rare. That's about how often some of us get em too. And look at me, driving this damn Cadillac and don't even have a savings account for my daughter's college education. Ain't had a vacation since we visited Salina's folks in Norfolk six years ago, and that was a drag anyway. I bet that sucker was in Europe last summer. I work my nuts off, lose six days a week to make money to survive, and can't say I liked one day, not one damn day.

She has empathy not only for her male characters but also for the women, who, unlike those in some novels, are not saintly martyrs surrounded by brutes. Very few of us are Mother Teresa, and the late Christopher Hitchens cited even her flaws.

Working-class men are up against it in a society where your melanin content and not the content of your character determines who gets ahead and who remains behind. Because he can't find a job, Langston in "Reconstruction" descends into alcoholism and paranoia. Langston is multidimensional in this masterpiece, one of the finest short stories in the American canon. Economic insecurity has made him mean. Unable to find work, he declines mentally, into distrust, and takes it out on his wife.

Scientists are finally taking seriously the subject of race, putting a critical eye on the consequences of sensational journalism, talk shows, and cheap profit-making entertainment—as a former CNN president said: "Race sells." In popular culture, Black peo-

ple take the rap for all of society's ills and white pathology is ignored. But science is starting to place the effects of this kind of
racism under a microscope. It's called the weathering hypothesis.
Public health researcher Arline Geronimus from the University
of Michigan says traditional beliefs that the disparities in white/
Black lifespan are due to genetics, diet, and exercise don't explain
data that's accumulated over the years. Instead, she makes the case
that marginalized people suffer nearly constant stress from living
with poverty and discrimination, which damages their bodies at
the cellular level and leads to increasingly serious health problems
over time.

It's members of McMillan's class who are harmed the most,
physically and psychologically. I've seen Black achievers, acquain-
tances of mine, die young from hypertension. Dr. Geronimus's
research has found that upward mobility and wealth aren't anti-
dotes for weathering. In one 2006 study, she analyzed the health
data—including blood pressure, cortisol levels, liver function, and
cholesterol—of more than 1,500 survey respondents and found
that high-income Black women had worse health outcomes than
low-income white women.

Some of McMillan's characters deal with this pain and hurt by
consuming alcohol. Others convert the pain into success. Be-
trayed by Richard, a co-worker, and even suffering a miscarriage,
Marilyn in "Quilting on the Rebound" sublimates her hurt by
becoming an entrepreneur.

> I began to patronize just about every fabric store in down-
> town Los Angeles, and while I listened to the humming
> of my machine, and concentrated on designs that I
> couldn't believe I was creating, it occurred to me that I
> wasn't suffering from heartache at all. I actually felt this
> incredible sense of relief. As if I didn't have to anticipate

anything else happening that was outside of my control. And when I did grieve, it was always because I had lost a child, not a future husband.

McMillan shows the energy and anxiety women expend in their efforts to please men who don't appreciate them, efforts that feel similar to filling out a job application or applying for an Ivy League school.

> For weeks I couldn't eat or sleep. At first, all I did was think about what was wrong with me. I was too old. For him. No. He didn't care about my age. It was the gap in my teeth, or my slight overbite, from all those years I used to suck my thumb. But he never mentioned anything about it and I was really the only one who seemed to no-tice. I was flat-chested. I had cellulite. My ass was square instead of round. I wasn't exciting as I used to be in bed. No. I was still good in bed, that much I did know. I couldn't cook. I was a terrible housekeeper. That was it. If you couldn't cook and keep a clean house, what kind of wife would you make?

For some reason, McMillan has been deprived of the prestige of those Black women writers endorsed by the "New York liter-ary establishment," which has directed trends in Black literature since the 1920s. The same could be said of the late Elizabeth Nunez, Paule Marshall, Louise Meriwether, Carlene Hatcher Polite, and others. Margaret Walker's novel *Jubilee* should cer-tainly be in contention for Great American Novel status, but she lived in Mississippi.

McMillan's work is highly crafted, having been workshopped at the Harlem Writers Guild and other writing laboratories. Her portrayal of intimacy is beyond realism. This passage from "Reconstruction" shows she could well be called the professor of intimacy.

> When I couldn't get his smell out of my nostrils or his scent off my body and didn't want to. I embarrassed myself many a day walking around sniffing my own wrists and shoulders, trying to get another whiff of him. Sometimes, during dictation, my mind would wander out over a skyscraper and there his face would be, filtering through a moving cloud. His skin was so smooth it looked like black ice. I could see the muscles in his long arms squeezing me like suctions. Could see his feet dangling over the end of the bed, and gliding up and down my legs. I got tingles all through my body and goosebumps up and down my arms just thinking about how mushy he made me feel.

Her scenes are camera-ready. Her submission to *The 1619 Project,* "From Behind the Counter," about a sit-in at a lunch counter, is superior to most documentaries about the subject. The documentaries would miss a character who is proud of the protesting students but would lose his job if he were to show his pride.

> By now, the waitresses was just ignoring them like they weren't even there. I wanted to say something to the young men but I was scared I would get fired. When I picked up the rubber tray full of dirty dishes and walked past them I did push a fork so it would fall on the floor and when I bent down to pick it up I locked eyes with all four of them and they could see I was proud.

She is able to replicate the dialogue of multiple characters. Her descriptions of culture, food, and fashion are meticulously represented. Here, in "Touching," is her eye roaming a block party:

> The block was starting to fill up with makeshift vendors displaying junk they'd pulled out of attics and closets and basements so that they wouldn't have to drag them to the Salvation Army. I could already smell barbecue and popcorn and hear the DJ testing his speakers for the highest quality of sound that he could expect to get from outside. It was very hot and the sun was beating down on the pavement, making the heat penetrate through your shoes.

The arbiters of Black fiction seem to feel that bestseller-dom and artistry are mutually exclusive. As Terry recalls in the same UC Berkeley commencement address:

> I never aspired to be on the *New York Times* bestseller list or to make millions of dollars from a book. The money's not bad, but it was not my goal. I wanted people to read my books so that they would feel better about themselves but it has taken a lot for me to feel good about myself. I wanted respect. I wanted my stories to make people feel valid. To give them strength, and perhaps courage. And that, to me, is worth far more than fame and money.

I would run into Terry occasionally: in Philadelphia, where she received the American Book Award for *Mama;* in Las Vegas, where I took a photo of her and her late mother; and at a *Poets & Writers* dinner. She was the same as she was when she was a student at Cal—unpretentious.

In 2021, she appeared via Zoom when she accepted the PEN

Oakland Award, called by the *New York Times* "the 'blue-collar' PEN awards," a nickname that feels appropriate for this writer whose roots are in the working class. She said in her acceptance speech for her novel *It's Not All Downhill from Here:*

> First, I'd like to say how grateful I am to receive this award from PEN Oakland for *It's Not All Downhill from Here,* and to be included and honored with such a wonderful group of writers. We all found our voices some time ago, and I'm just glad that we did. I write stories about women who don't know how strong they are until they fall or are pushed down, and are trying to find their way back up after they've lost it. I wrote *Downhill* when I was in my sixties because I was under the impression that life was all downhill after sixty, but I found out that wasn't true.
>
> I'm now seventy, and I don't feel any different than I did when I was sixty. Well, that's not true. But the point is, I'm grateful to still have my eyes on the future and not worry about what's behind me, but what may still lie ahead . . . What I do know is that we have right now, and I'm happy to share it with all of you. I do not write to prove anything. I write to discover a new truth or many truths.

And though her skills in delineating the pico and the micro are often brilliant, this author is capable of cosmic thinking. It was published nearly fifty years ago, but "The End" feels prophetic when she writes:

> In his dream it was worse than the thirties. It had to be. The country was in a big bind, and everybody was freaking scared, almost to the point of leaving. But there was

nowhere to go. Everybody was having internal and external problems with other nations. They were all fighting for the same thing. Power. Control. Money. They couldn't see how impossible it was to sustain all three without the likelihood of war. But that was another thing that had been conspired by all the nations. War was the safest and most undetectable form of genocide.

Like she reads her characters, in this passage, she reads the times we're living through.

Ishmael Reed
Oakland, California

Ishmael Reed is a novelist, poet, songwriter, jazz pianist, composer, illustrator, magazine publisher, editor, and book publisher. He has received honors and awards in the United States, Japan, China, and Europe. His most recent novel, *The Terrible Fives,* was published in 2025 by Baraka Books.

Write Fast and Hard, She Said

Kristine Bell

Twenty-five years ago, Terry McMillan's refrigerator repairman asked her why she was writing her own check for the repair. Her response, "I need a new assistant," prompted a chain of events resulting in *It Was the Way She Said It: Short Stories, Essays, and Wisdom* by Terry McMillan.

It was 2000, and I was a freshly minted English major from Mills College. As soon as I had my degree in my hand, I devoured *Mama* and *Waiting to Exhale*. A steady diet of Shakespeare and Virginia Woolf had me hungry for the voices of real folks living lives I could relate to. Having grown up in a rough neighborhood, I was not wrong to be intimidated by the possibility of working with a woman whose books had the power to make the publishing industry take notice.

A white twenty-something from Richmond, California, I wasn't her typical fan, and that was important to her. My office was a cozy room in her custom-built ranch home, open and spacious, each room curated with furniture and art like a museum.

Her office was warm. Books stacked floor to ceiling, and walls covered with the *New York Times* bestseller lists that featured her books. Nervous and excited by the opportunity to impress her with my smarts, I did my best to underpromise and overdeliver. After a few weeks she invited me into her office and asked me to sit down. She swiveled around from her computer and straightened a stack of papers. I was nervous. She said, "I want you to hear this." A million scenarios raced through my head in an instant: Was this it? Was she going to fire me? I held my breath and braced myself for the worst. She cleared her throat, tilted her head, and started reading her latest manuscript.

Since that afternoon, she's read to me more times than I could count. I don't even remember what she read, but it became clear my responsibilities were more than phones and filing. She relied on me to make sure she had the time and space she needed to bring real people and real experiences to life on the page.

It was as much fun as it was work. She taught me the importance of prioritizing organization as well as connection and communication with the people who support you along your journey. I had no idea of the immense value those lessons and skills would have in our future.

The years since have pulled us in different directions. I've enjoyed a corporate career and I write, as well as maintain her online presence. When the opportunity to support a collection of her short fiction came up, nervous and excited, I jumped at the chance.

Bringing *It Was the Way She Said It* to life has been an honor and a pleasure. Despite the tedium of flipping through paper files, scanning thousands of pages of fragile documents from as far back as the seventies and eighties, plus formatting the alphabet soup that each digital document came up with, the chance to bring young Terry's words out of the files and into readers' hands was worth it.

Most of the pieces in *It Was the Way She Said It* showcase Terry McMillan's journey to becoming the writer we all know, her voice *before* her blockbuster success. The collection introduces Terry McMillan, a short-story writer pouring her heart and soul out onto the page. Each piece is a step in her evolution toward becoming an author who, despite record-breaking book sales, remains an underappreciated American voice.

In the pages that follow you will see how she tried things out and learned to trust her own voice by following her characters' leads. Aware that I've always wanted to write novels, she was generous with her knowledge. She once shared, "You should let your notes and other ideas pile up while you're writing. You will be shocked at how gratifying this process is and how much you learn about the characters and the story if you listen to THEM instead of thinking about how good or bad what you've written is."

The book is organized in sections:

• *Published fiction* that dates from as far back as 1976, when she was in college, to 2019.

• *Unpublished fiction* from her personal files dating back to the early 1980s, when she supported herself as a freelance word processor. When she wasn't working, she was writing and submitting her work to magazines—*The Atlantic* (rejected), *Ms.* magazine (rejected), *Essence* magazine (accepted as a columnist after winning a contest)—as well as literary journals (she was published in *Callaloo, River Styx,* and *Coydog Review*), and attending Mac-Dowell and Yaddo writers' residencies. Terry wasn't going to let money, love, or a few rejections stop her.

• *Sketches and starts* that show her experimenting with craft and character, short pieces taken from her personal files, and excerpts from a novel in progress.

• *Essays, speeches, and opinions* that highlight her nonfiction voice, as authentic and truthful as her complicated characters. Though many are more than thirty years old, the topics and truth-telling land as if they were addressing current events.

These works span a fifty-year timeline, probing topics that are controversial and sensitive—some of which are difficult to stomach today. It is important that readers note the shifting cultural and generational contexts that each piece was born from. Present-day editorial changes were limited to grammar, punctuation, factual accuracy, and readability; care was taken to preserve the original voice and style of Terry as a developing writer. This collection was shaped by a variety of source materials: Terry's personal collection of files; correspondence and draft versions of stories to and from her early reader and friend Virginia Dunwell; college friends and mentors like Ishmael Reed; the archives of UC Berkeley, where she published her first articles as a journalism student writing for *Black Thoughts;* and the Harlem Writers Guild.

Though each piece comes to the collection from a different phase of the writing process, all of them bear the Terry McMillan signature voice. And just like it did the first time she ever read to me, Terry's voice transports me right into the world she's created. I hope these stories do the same for you.

Kristine Bell is a writer, editor, producer, and bookseller at Point Reyes Books.

IT WAS
THE WAY
SHE SAID IT

PUBLISHED
FICTION

McMillan's first fiction publication was in 1976 while she was an undergraduate at UC Berkeley. She was a journalism major, known then as Terri McMillan. Her creative writing professor, MacArthur Fellow Ishmael Reed, told her she had a distinctive voice. The short story "The End" was published in *Yardbird Reader* volume 5 alongside luminaries Amiri Baraka, Quincy Troupe, Ernest Gaines, Gayl Jones, and others.

The End

[1976]

It is seven A.M., Monday morning. Detroit's lower east side is still. Pobre Blackstone turns off the alarm and lets his head drop back deep into his pillow. Another day another dollar. Ford Motor Company's assembly line is waiting for him to show up, punch the clock, and do his time for the day. Dammit, better get up. He has felt the same way each morning for the past twelve years.

Forgetting to brush his teeth or comb his hair thoroughly, Pobre runs out into the brisk morning air and waits for his 1973 Cadillac to warm up. Pobre's legs aren't as long as he'd like them to be so he has to pull the seat up as far as it will go. He doesn't look like the Cadillac type with his short dumpy frame, but he handles the car with grace. He looks more like a Mustang Man, you'd think. He's handsome enough to get away with a Cadillac because when he takes his Sunday afternoon drives, all the women on the street turn in wonder at this handsome creature in the gold Coupe de Ville.

He turns on the soulful FM station for some music to heat his body, but the news is on instead. Let me see what's up today, Pobre says out loud. Nixon's dead!? Hallelujah, the sorry mutha fucka shoulda been dead, long time ago. People are in mourning but are going to work anyway. What was it they said he had? Phlebitis or some shit? Turns out he committed suicide and no one can understand why for the life of them. Turn the station. This is too morbid and funny at the same time. AM. That's more like it, and one of his favorite tunes accompanies him toward the freeway.

Every dull ass morning I drive the same dull ass way, wear the same dull ass uniform, and feel the same dull ass way going to this lousy job. And look at that old bitch over there. Got enough hairspray in her hair to starch a laundry of clothes. She can afford to bleach her hair to lightening frightening blond and tease it so everybody can see it cause she's rich. In her Mercedes-Benz, bitch. All them honkies is rich, including the women. This must be her neighbor behind her. Seems like rich people don't mind tailgating each other. But if it was me behind em, they'd change lanes. I'd like to run into one of em and get me some insurance, something ugly. I bet that dude is in Ford's office from eight to five, and I bet he has clean fingernails, and I bet he loves his job. I bet he doesn't mind getting up in the morning. He can drink coffee and eat doughnuts all day and have lunch with the fellas. Probably drinks wine with his lunch and eats his steaks rare. That's about how often some of us get em too. And look at me, driving this damn Cadillac and don't even have a savings account for my daughter's college education. Ain't had a vacation since we visited Salina's folks in Norfolk six years ago, and that was a drag anyway. I bet that sucker was in Europe last summer. I work my nuts off, lose six days a week to make money to survive, and can't say I liked one day, not one damn day.

He parks the car in the lot filled with thousands of automobiles. He tries to count the Fords but hardly any are visible. *Good. At least all of us aren't as stupid and dedicated as they think we are. Here comes Gus, smiling his ass off, and I wonder what makes this man so damn cheerful every morning coming to this Giant Machine.*

"Hey, what's happening, Gus? Why don't you wipe that smirky smile off your face and be serious? I can't smile when I get up: can't think of one good reason to. One day I'm gonna wake up and say fuck Ford Motor Company, you know what I mean, man? Doesn't this job, this place, just make you want to vomit sometimes?"

"Here we go again, you know darn well it's alright here, man. The pay is good, benefits are excellent, overtime is great, and, besides, where will you ever get a three-week vacation after working two years in a place? You niggers are all alike. Never satisfied with anything but sex. What's wrong, didn't you get any last night?"

Gus Nixon, a twenty-nine-year-old country boy, looks down at Pobre and taps him on the shoulder. Gus doesn't complain about his job. After eight years in the navy, he sees Ford's assembly line as somewhat of a relaxing atmosphere. He doesn't have to exert any mental energy like he did then. He just collects his check every Friday, gets drunk on the weekends, and smiles. These are his plans for the next thirty years. Ford has a family plan that Gus is crazy about because it has fit his needs perfectly. What's to complain about?

Pobre follows him, smiling with his eyes at this fool, but with a serious look on his face, bolts out, "Man, if you weren't my only white friend, I'd kick your ass for saying that shit. I can never be satisfied with a dull ass job like this, and, if you are, then you're not as intelligent as the rest of your race, you're a stupid man. Can't you do anything else? You shouldn't be here noway.

If it wasn't for your godfathers I probably wouldn't be here now. All the rest of your people got every damn thing. What's your problem? I know you didn't dream of growing up to be a Ford's play toy, or did you? This job is enough to drain all your guts dry. No. Hell no! I'm not satisfied with this job. As long as I have to get up every morning when I don't want to, as long as my paycheck keeps getting bigger and buying less, man, I can't be satisfied. If I was, then I'd be just like you. Now, we can't let that happen, can we?"

The two men laugh it off and go their separate ways. Pobre walks past rows and rows of gray and black machines until he gets to his own personal spot. It is already in operating order because the man on the night shift has just gone home. Swissh. Shzzz. Swisssh. Shzzzz. All the machines are holding their daily arguments, each seeing who can be the loudest. Pobre has gotten used to the noise, but he hears nothing as he puts the first steel wedge into its socket. This wedge is the embryo of a car door. *I hope all the doors fall off before it leaves the plant.* But they won't. They never do, never have, and if they did, he wouldn't be there today.

If this were the pickle factory, I could just spit in the jars or something, but here there isn't much I could get away with without getting jammed. I used to crack up when Salina told me how they used to flick cigarette ashes in the jars, put buggers in em, and anything else they could find. They hated that job. I guess everybody hates their job.

As Pobre begins his daily ritual, his mind goes blank. This happens every morning. This is when he can get his thoughts out of his system because he doesn't have to use his brain to run a stupid machine. Pobre's mind begins to drift to last night's dream or nightmare, and he goes over it again in his head.

In his dream it was worse than the thirties. It had to be. The country was in a big bind, and everybody was freaking scared, almost to the point of leaving. But there was nowhere to go. Everybody was having internal and external problems with other nations. They were all fighting for the same thing. Power. Control. Money. They couldn't see how impossible it was to sustain all three without the likelihood of war. But that was another thing that had been conspired by all the nations. War was the safest and most undetectable form of genocide.

Even on the domestic front things were taking on the shape of total societal perversion. Men no longer screwed women. Everyone smoked packs of cigarettes a day and bought Valiums in supermarkets for their nerves. Women and men had begun negotiations for a civil war for the same reasons that the nations were battling over. Power. Religious fanatics were all making concessions and preparations for the day the whole world would end because they said it would be any day now. They had foreseen it long ago. It was true, though. Every traumatic incident had taken place and shape in the past five years, and it was just one big scene after another.

The government had initiated a new program called Project Search. It was geared toward capturing all Black people under thirty who were not educated and making them slaves to the government. They all had guaranteed jobs, a place to stay, and good pensions. It created more jobs that people didn't like but did anyway. All for the same reasons. They didn't understand what was going on at all. No one did. They just did what they were told and asked no questions. Had a good time.

Things were bad. It seemed as if the Bible was telling the truth after all. Universal Studios recently had gotten a federal grant to turn it into a movie so that in case it was finished before the world ended, everyone would be able to understand why. The movie would be free. Who cared?

On the six, seven, and eight o'clock news, a nervous voice

stated the following: "Well, folks, this will be the last newscast for all eternity. Today's the day. The founders of this land, this world, have given up. Each nation has become so overwhelmed with problems they have exhausted their resources for solutions. They candidly state that the problems are too complex to solve and that each of them is so interrelated it would take forever to straighten things out. At this point in time, they don't rightly know themselves what could straighten things out, and, if it could, they don't know how they would be able to tell if things were straightened out. They all had a conference at the United Nations last night and came to a general consensus: Fuck it, just fuck it. Therefore, at eleven o'clock, say your last prayers and spend these last precious days or hours reminiscing about your lives. Think about what it has meant to you and what you have accomplished in it. Many of us will have to agree that it was not all in vain. We have learned to cope with pain so this shouldn't be any worse. Personally, I wish to extend my sincere hopes that all of you folks out there will find some peace somewhere after this is over. And for those of you who have learned your lesson well by what those in power have done to our world, perhaps next time you can help avoid this kind of mess again. Good luck, goodbye, and good night."

It is lunchtime and Pobre's brow is sweating ferociously. *Damn, that's why I'm so irritable today, huh? Hell, it was only a stupid dream. But what about life? Is it really that absurd? It feels just like reality. Nothin surprises me anymore. The people in power are capable of doing anything, especially things that do more harm for us than good. People like me. I better start paying closer attention to the news to see what is going to happen next.*

Pobre is back in the fine brick home that cost him $8,500 when he bought it twelve years ago. It's now worth $22,000. It is filled with the finest furniture his paycheck could buy. Salina has just finished looking at the four-thirty movie. "Hi, honey. The food is on the stove, and Nostalgia is in the basement playing. You tired? Want me to rub your neck and ankles for you? You look beat, or worried. Something wrong?"

"No, honey," as he caresses her behind. "I just got some serious thinking to do. I gotta start thinking about the future, our future, everybody's future. I had this crazy ass dream last night about the world coming to an end, and shit, it's been bugging me all day."

"Pobre, don't let no silly dream start messing up your head now. Dreams don't mean nothing. The world's gotta end one day anyway, so let it happen on its own course. Nostalgia's kid's kid's kids will probably be around, maybe more than that. We gonna be here a long time, less you worries all of us to death bout some crazy dream. I got something to ease the tension for you, why don't you go lie down, and I'll be in in a minute."

He slips off his work boots in the middle of the living room floor, drops his overcoat on the chair, and sits down. He doesn't really feel like making love, not right now. "Honey, would you get me a beer, please? That'll be enough for my nerves right now, okay? Nothing personal, honey, just one of them days."

Salina is a thirty-two-year-old Southern beauty. She had the roundest ass Pobre had ever seen, and he used to pour ice water on it just to see it roll off and watch her nipples rise. After five years of marriage, Nostalgia was born and has the same chocolate skin as her father, and the same bone structure as her mother.

Nostalgia comes running into the living room and stands beside her father. "Hi, Daddy. Wanna see what I wrote today?" Before he can answer, she pulls out a neatly folded piece of notebook paper. Pobre opens it and reads out loud:

" 'Dear God: My mama cries when Daddy goes to hard work. She is scared for Daddy. Mama says everything be worse and we might go to the poorhouse. Please, God, don't let everything be worse. Mama, Daddy, and me don't want to go nowhere. Love, Nostalgia.'"

Pobre's heart is beating too fast. He feels his puffy face flush and flutter. The blood seems to fall from his head to his feet, and he just looks at Nostalgia with a mixture of strength and pity. Who had told her God could solve all the problems, and Lord, this child was smart enough to think about writing God for help. Pobre doesn't know what to say. He doesn't know Salina had been tripping on the same things his dream had conveyed. It may have been a little exaggerated version of reality, but it wasn't far off.

"Honey, Daddy ain't going nowhere, none of us are. And I'll work until ain't no such thing as work. If God gets this letter in time, maybe everything will get better. Now go tell your mama to come here so we can help love her a little more so she won't be crying when I go to hard work, okay?"

"Okay, Daddy." Nostalgia runs into the kitchen to get her mother and finds her leaning against the refrigerator in tears. "Mama, Daddy said come here so he can love you." She hugs her mama around the thighs and Salina holds her hand as they walk into the living room.

Pobre hears tears before he can turn to see them. He pulls her to him and holds her as if it were the last day on earth. They all cry until they can't cry anymore. They all know then that no matter what is to come into their lives, there is nothing they can do but love each other and keep on loving each other. They would do just that.

The news that evening resembles statements one would normally associate with science fiction movies. Out of this world.

. . . At the Vladivostok summit, it was the intention of President Ford and Chairman Brezhnev to lay plans to work hard for an agreement on the further limitation of nuclear strategic weapons.

. . . Mideast . . . torn by new rounds of terrorism and reprisal between Arabs and Israelis. Both sides must decide on new moves toward peace or more war.

. . . Mideast . . . If pushed too far, the U.S. will be forced to choose between economic ruin and armed action if Arab oil supplies are not secured in time to eliminate an international disaster. Could be early as 1976.

. . . Western Europe: As Russia encourages its Communist parties, the U.S. is watching its allies trying to deal with inflation, strikes, the energy crisis, and the gradual decline of the quality of human life.

. . . Italy . . . is in desperate straits, awaiting action by its thirty-seventh government in thirty-one years. Inflation rate is 25 percent annually. Vital imports take a billion dollars a month more than Italy earns. A million Italians are jobless: Many only work part-time. The West's biggest Communist party is waiting.

. . . Britain . . . also is running a billion-dollar deficit abroad each month. Prime Minister Wilson says Britain faces its greatest crisis since World War II.

. . . France . . . is plunging into economic recession and social strife. A wave of strikes by workers in state-run industries deprived the French of mail for six weeks and garbage collections for a week.

. . . Just ahead . . . not only in France, but elsewhere in Western Europe, you can expect a three-way struggle. Part of Western Europe wants to work closely with the U.S. as an essential ally. Part wants to keep the U.S. at arm's length while trying to make Western Europe the "third superpower," united and equal to the U.S. and Russia. A relative few want Western Europe to line up with Russia.

The telephone interrupts the news report, and Pobre goes to answer it. It is Gus. "Hello, Pobre?"

"Yeah, Gus, how you doing, what's happening, man?"

"Man, you won't believe this. Those sons of bitches laid me off today. Would you believe that? I knew I should've stayed in the navy. At least they treated me like a human being. Man, I don't know what I'm gonna do now, not the slightest idea. Unemployment won't pay my rent, and the car note and food and hell, man, I got two kids. What is a guy supposed to do when shit like this happens, just what kind of alternatives does a guy have? If I saw that Ford character I'd piss in his eyeballs and shit in his face and see how he likes it. Pobre, you were right, man. Ford is so fucked up it's pitiful.

"I just wanted to let you know you won't be seeing me in the parking lot tomorrow, man. Take it easy, and I'll keep in touch, man."

Pobre said his goodbyes and hung up the phone. *Too bad it happens like this. I never thought I'd live to see a day when everything was so mixed up like a big crossword puzzle and none of the pieces seem to fit. I wonder what the world will be like for Nostalgia.*

It is seven A.M., Monday morning, and Pobre Blackstone turns off the alarm. He decides to go back to sleep. He's tired.

After UC Berkeley, McMillan enjoyed success as a freelance writer, writing articles and essays that called on her journalism training, including a column in *Essence* magazine. Almost nine years after her first fiction publication, McMillan was published again, in the 1985 Erotic Humor issue of the *Coydog Review*. Written with the working title "Touching Is Serious," but published as "Touching," this story shows the earliest expression of the voice she will become known for: raw and vulnerable, real and humorous.

Touching

[1985]

I suspected someone was there in that very same spot before me, but I didn't let the thought grow in my mind or rot there, till I saw her swinging on your side like a shoulder-strap purse early this morning. And this was after I had already let you touch me all over with your long brown hands and break down my resistance, so that you left me feeling like the earth had been pulled from under my feet.

First saw your lean long legs coming toward me on that crooked gray sidewalk, the silver specks glaring in my eyes like dancing stars. But I was not blinded, even when you dragged them in that elegant, yet pompous kinda way of yours. And you watched me coming from at least a half a block away and those size 13s didn't seem to lift up off the cement as high as they did the other night when we walked down this very same street to-gether.

I know it was me who called you up the other night to say hello, but it was you who invited me to come down and walk your dog with you. Sounded innocent enough to me, but all along I'm sure you knew that I wanted to finally find out how warm it was under your shirt, behind your zipper, and if your hands were as gentle and strong as they looked. I was really hoping we could skip the walk altogether cause I just wanted to fall down on you slowly and get to your insides. Walk the dog another time. But since you could've misconstrued my motives as being unladylike, I bounced on down the street to your apartment in my white jogging outfit, trying to look as alluring as I possibly could, but without looking too eager.

I even dabbed gold oil behind my ears, under each breast, and on the tips of my elbows so as to lure you closer to me in case you couldn't make up your own mind. The truth of the matter is that I was nervous because I knew that we weren't gonna just chitchat tonight like we'd done before. I went out of my way in five minutes flat to brush my teeth twice, put on fresh coats of red lipstick, wash under my arms, Q-tip my ears and navel (cause I didn't know just how far you might want to go), and wash in my most intimate areas and sprinkle a little jasmine oil there too.

Even though it was almost ninety degrees, we walked fifteen blocks and the dog didn't let go of anything. You didn't seem to mind or notice. You handed me the leash, and even though I can't stand to see a grown man with a little cutesy-wutesy dog, I wasn't hostile as I tugged at it as we continued to walk through the thick night air. For the most part, I like dogs.

When our feet dropped from the curb, and I jumped and screamed because a fallen leaf looked like a dead mouse, I let go of the leash and grabbed your hand. You squeezed it back, though you had to drag me to chase after your dog, who had taken off down the sidewalk, running up to the trees' bark and just panting. When we finally caught him, we were both out of breath. I regretted wearing that sweaty jogging suit.

"You scared of a little mouse?" you asked.

"Yes, they give me the heebie-jeebies. My stomach turns over and I want to jump on top of chairs and stuff just to get away from them."

Then you told me about the time you busted one on your kitchen counter eating your ravioli right out the can and how you wounded it with a broomstick and then tried to flush it down the toilet, but it wouldn't flush. I laughed loud and hard, but I wanted to make you laugh too.

So, I told you about the time I was on my way out of my house to take a sauna when I accidentally saw a giant roach cavorting on my kitchen counter. I whacked it with my right hand just hard enough to cripple it. (I am scared of mice but I hate roaches.) I didn't want it to die immediately because I had just spent $9.95 on some Roach-Proof which I had ordered through the newspaper and wanted to see if it really worked. So, sprinkled about a quarter teaspoon on his head as he was about to struggle to find a crack or crevice somewhere. He kept on trying so I kept on sprinkling more Proof on his antennae. After five minutes of this, he was getting on my nerves cause I still had my coat on, my purse and gym bag thrown over my shoulders, and since my kitchen was designed strictly with dwarfs and children in mind, I was burning up. It was then that I decided to burn him up too. First I lit myself a cigarette, and with the same match, burned off his antennae but the sucker still kept trying to get to one corner of the counter. I got real mad because my Proof was obviously not working and I just went ahead and burnt him up quickly and totally for not dying the way he was supposed to.

*

You thought this was terribly funny and cracked up. I liked hearing you laugh, but I didn't know if you thought this was indicative of my personality: torture and murder and everything.

We continued to walk a few more blocks, making small talk, and the dog continued running up to tree trunks, kicking up his little white legs, and finally squirting out wetness, but that was about it.

By this time, I was sweating and picturing your head nestled between my breasts. I like feeling a man's head there, and it had been so long since any man even made me feel like dreaming out loud, that I didn't even hear you when you asked me if I liked the Temptations and had I ever been to a puppet show. I didn't understand the connection until we walked inside your apartment.

Today, though, you watched me come toward you like this was a tug-of-war, but the rope was invisible. The gravity was so dense that it pulled us face-to-face and when I finally reached you, I could smell your breath at the end of the rope. You were uneasy, and sorta turned in a half-turn toward me as I brushed past both of you. You loosely smiled back at me, squinting behind those tinted glasses, and I smiled back at both of you cause I don't have a grudge with this girl; wasn't her who I spent the night with.

"What are you doing up so early?" you asked. I didn't really think it was any of your business since you didn't call last night to see how late I was up. Besides, it was almost ten o'clock in the morning.

"I've already had my coffee, done my laundry, and now I'm trying to get to the plant store to buy some dirt so I can transplant my fern and rubber tree before the block party this afternoon."

"Oh, I'm sorry, Marie, this is Carolyn," you said, waving your hands between us like a magician.

We both nodded like ladies, fully understanding your uneasiness.

"Why don't you have the Chinese people do your laundry?" you asked.

"Because I like to know that my clothes are clean; I like to fold them up nice and neat like I want them. And besides, I like to put things together that belong together."

You just nodded your head like a fool. For a moment you looked puzzled, like someone had dropped you off in the middle of nowhere. You didn't seem to mind either that the girl was standing there watching your poise alter and sway. Me neither. But I had to move away from you cause I could really smell your body scent now and it was starting to stick to my skin, gravitating around me, until it got all up into my nostrils and then hit my brain, swelled up my whole head right there on the spot. This was embarrassing, so I tried to play it off by pulling my scarlet scarf down closer toward my eyebrows. But you already knew what had happened.

I made my feet move away from you as if I was trying to catch a bus I saw approaching. I took my hands and wiped away the burnt-red lipstick from my mouth and cheeks at the mere thought of letting you press yours against them. Was trying to forget how handsome you were altogether. Fine. Too fine. Too fine. Didn't listen to my mama. "Never look at a man that's prettier than you, cause he's gonna act that way." I was trying to think about dirt. The leaves of my plants. But I never have been attracted to pretty men, I thought, trying to miss the cracks in the sidewalk after stubbing my toe. You were different. Spoke correct English. Made puppets move and talk. Wrote your own grant proposals. Drank herbal tea and didn't smoke cigarettes. You crossed your legs and arms when you talked, and leaned your wide shoulders back in your chair so your behind slid to the edge. Made me think you thought about the words before letting them roll off your tongue. I admired you for contemplating things before you made them happen.

You yelled at me after I was almost halfway down the block. "Are you selling anything at the block party?"

I had already told you the other day I was making zucchini cake, but I repeated it again. "Zucchini cake!" and waved good-bye, trying to keep that stupid grin on my face though I knew you wouldn't have been able to see my expression from a distance.

I liked the attention you were giving me in spite of the girl. I thought it meant something. I was even hoping as I trucked into the plant store and got stuck by a cactus that you would call me later on to explain that she was just a friend or your cousin or your sister. I was hoping that you would tell me that your back hurt or something so I could come down with my almond oil and rub it for you. Beat it, dig my fingertips into your shoulder blades and the canals along your spine until you gave in. Or maybe you would tell me you broke your glasses and couldn't see. I would come down and read out loud to you: comic books or the Bible.

Now I'm out here on this sidewalk with a bag of black dirt in my hands in the heat walking past your house, forcing myself not to stare up at those dingy white shutters of yours so I twist my neck in the opposite direction, looking ridiculous and completely conspicuous. I thought for sure I was gonna be your one-and-only-down-the-street sweetheart, cause I carried myself like a lady, not like some dog in heat.

I really had no intention of transplanting anything today. I just told you that because it sounded clean. I was more concerned about whether this girl touched you last night the way I had. Probably not, because only I can touch you the way I touch you.

But as you were standing there on that sidewalk, I kept seeing still shots of us flashing across my eyes: twisting inside each other's arms like worms and caterpillars; you kissing me like you'd been getting paid for it all these years and this was your last paycheck; and my head getting lost all over your body. I could still hear your faint cries echoing in my head right there on that concrete. Saw my tongue moistening your chest and your hands rubbing all across and around my back like I was made of silk. I was silk and you knew it. You smelled so damn good. And you never stopped me when my head fell off the bed. You came after it. You never said anything when I screamed and called out your name, just took your time with me and kept pulling me inside your arms, inside the cave of your chest, and would not let me go. And when I woke up, you were the dream I thought I had.

And yet, there you were out on that sidewalk in the heat with another girl chained to your arm, walking past my house without a care in the world. This shit burns me up.

I mean look. You didn't have to make me laugh out loud, tickle me, and change the Band-Aid on my cut thumb, or sniff my hair and tell me it smelled like a cool forest. You didn't have to tell me it didn't matter that my breasts were small, and I was relieved to hear that, cause my mama always told me that a man should be more interested in how you fill his life and not how you fill your bra.

I mean who told you to show me the puppets you'd made of James Brown and Diana Ross and the Jackson Five? Who told you to burn jasmine candles and make me listen to twelve old Temptations records after telling me your favorite one of all was "Ain't Too Proud to Beg"? You didn't have to climb up on a bar stool and drag out your scrapbook and give me the privilege of seeing four generations of your family. Showing me your picture as a little nappy-headed boy. What made you think I wanted to see you as a child when I'd really only known you as a man for three weeks? But no, you watched me turn my key in my front door for two whole months while you walked that little mutt before you allowed yourself to say more than "hello" and "good morning."

I never did get around to explaining myself, did I? I mean, I think I told you I was a special education teacher. I think I told you that once in a while I write poems. Even wrote one for you but I'm glad I didn't give it to you. Your ego probably would've popped out of your chest. But maybe I should've told you about the nights when my head pumps no blood, and about the dreams I have of being loved just so. How I have always wanted to give a man more than a symphony inside and outside the bedroom. But it is so hard. Look at this.

You just should not have wrapped your arms and shoulders around me like I was your firstborn child. You should not have shown me tenderness and passion. Was this just lust? I mean, I wasn't asleep when you kept on touching and rubbing my face like I was crystal and you were afraid I would break. I pretended because I didn't want you to rupture this cocoon I was inside of. So I just let you touch; never wanted you to stop touching me.

Three hours ago I transplanted my plants anyway. I baked three zucchini cakes that cost me almost thirty dollars but after this morning I cannot picture myself sitting out on those cement steps in the heat trying to sell a piece of cake to total strangers. My roommate said she didn't mind. And I'm not going to sit in this hot house all day and be miserable.

"Wanna meet me for brunch?" I ask a girlfriend. She has no money. "I'll pay, just meet me, girl, okay?" She understands that I'm not really hungry but will eat anything just to take up inside space and get me away from this street.

The block was starting to fill up with makeshift vendors displaying junk they'd pulled out of attics and closets and basements so that they wouldn't have to drag them to the Salvation Army. I could already smell barbecue and popcorn and hear the DJ testing his speakers for the highest quality of sound that he could expect to get from outside. It was very hot and the sun was beating down on the pavement, making the heat penetrate through your shoes.

I'm wearing my tightest blue jeans and think I look especially good this afternoon on my way to the train station. I work hard to look good. Not for you or the general public, but for me. Here you come again, strutting toward me with that sissy little dog tagging alongside your big feet, but this time there's nothing on your arm but soft black hair and a rolled-up red plaid shirtsleeve. I can see orchards of black hair peeking out at me from your chest and though my knees want to buckle, I dig my heels deeply into the leather so as to make myself stand up straight like a dancer. You smile at me before we meet face-to-face and then do one of your about-face turns. Start walking beside me without even being invited.

"Hello," I say, as I make sure I don't lose the pace of my stride I worked so hard on establishing when I first noticed you.

"My goodness, you do look pretty today. Pink and purple are definitely your colors."

I smile because I know I look good and even though I can hardly breathe from holding my stomach in to look its absolute flattest, I don't want you staring at anything on my body too tough because you've seen far too much of it already. I take that back. I want you to be mesmerized by this sight so that you remember what everything looked and felt like underneath this denim because you won't be anywhere near that close again: daytime or nighttime. I move closer to the curb.

"Where you going today?" you ask, showing some real interest. And since I want you to think I'm a very busy woman and that this little episode has not fazed me in the least, I say, "I'm having brunch with a friend." I really wanted to tell you it wasn't any of your damn business, but no, I'm not only polite, but honest.

We walked six hard hot blocks and when we finally reached the subway steps, you bent down like you were about to kiss me, and I stared at your smooth brown lips puckering up as if you had a cold sore on them, and turned my head. You kissed that girl this morning.

"Can I call you later, then?" you asked.

"If the spirit moves you," I said, and disappeared underground.

By the time I got home it was almost ten o'clock and the street was still full of teenagers roller-skating, skateboarding, and dancing to the loud disco music blasting from both ends of the block. Kids were running around and through a full-spraying fire hydrant screaming high shrills of excitement, while grown-ups sat on the stoops sipping beers and drinks from Styrofoam cups. My roommate was sitting on our stoop and I joined her. Though it was hard to see, I found myself looking for your tall body over all the other smaller ones. When I didn't see you immediately, this disturbed me because I could see your lights on and I knew you couldn't be sitting up in that muggy apartment with all this noise and activity going on down here.

When I saw you leaning against a wrought iron fence across the street, there was a different girl stuck deep into your side. You spotted me through the thick crowd of teenagers and I heard you call out my name, but I ignored you. I was too proud to let myself feel sad or jealous or anything stupid like that.

My roommate told me she sold exactly three pieces of my zucchini cake because folks were afraid to buy it. Thought it might be green inside. I didn't care about the loss.

I felt spry and spunky, so I kicked off my pink pumps and marched down the steps and walked straight into the fanning water of the fire hydrant along with the kids. The hard mist felt cool and soothing as it fell against my skin. My entire body was tingling as if I had just had a massage. And even though I could feel your eyes following me, I didn't turn to acknowledge them. I sat back down on the steps, wiped the water from my forehead, the hot-pink lipstick from my lips, ate a piece of my delicious zucchini cake, and popped the lid on an ice-cold beer. The foam flowed over the top of the bottle and down my fingers. I shook off the excess, and leaned back against the cement step so it would scratch my back when I rocked from side to side and popped my fingers to the beat.

Released in spring 1986 in the literary journal *River Styx,* "Reconstruction" explores themes that set the stage for McMillan's second novel, the 1989 classic *Disappearing Acts,* whose central couple, Franklin and Zora, shares many of the same struggles featured here. In this story, the characters Langston and Lola are the embodiment of McMillan's seemingly endless curiosity about the tension and conflict of intimate relationships and her commitment to writing from the heart. Her refusal to shy away from difficult topics is reflected in her graphic depictions of sexual assault and domestic violence.

Reconstruction

[1986]

Langston got laid off.

I figured a week, maybe two weeks at most, he'd be back somewhere plastering. I told him, "Baby, don't worry, we can make it on my salary until you get called back or find something else." He shrugged his shoulders.

"I don't like the idea of living off a woman, even if you are my wife."

But that was six weeks ago, and our savings have disappeared by the week. We'd been saving almost a year for a house. We wanted to move away from this ugly city. Have some babies. Plant a garden in the earth in our backyard with stalks of corn, plump red tomatoes, bumpy yellow squash, and snapping green beans. Right now I feel good if I can dream about roses.

All he knows is construction, and the paper only asks for people who've got degrees in engineering and architecture. Langston didn't quite finish high school. But he reads.

"Langston, baby, why don't you try doing something else besides construction? You're no dummy, can't you find something else?"

"Like what?"

"Well, Glenda's husband is out of work too, and he took a job as a messenger."

"Be serious, Lola. You know how much they make? Minimum wage."

"Well, it's better than what you're making now, don't you think?"

"Look, stop comparing me to what other folks are doing, okay? What's a couple of hundred dollars gonna do for us after taxes? Huh?"

It'd mean the difference between bluefish and red snapper, half-and-half and homogenized milk in our coffee, and it'd mean he could buy his own cigarettes instead of smoking up all of mine.

"I'm going down to the Organization Monday morning, don't worry, I'll find something."

The Organization is a federally funded place that tries to get minorities and women jobs in construction. In this part of Brooklyn, it's called A Dream Deferred; in the Bronx, they've got A Change Is Gonna Come; in Queens, A Laying On of Hands; in Manhattan, Fight Back; and in Staten Island, Free at Last. Langston had told me that construction companies didn't like to hire Blacks and Spanish-speaking folks. Didn't want them in the union. I didn't want to believe him. But on my lunch hour, I began to notice the hundreds of hard hats building skyscrapers, sitting along the sidewalk drinking beer, eating heros and potato chips, and could count on two hands the brown faces I saw.

Last spring, Langston was with Fight Back. It was a real big mess at this hotel they were building on Seventh Avenue. It was all on the news and in the papers just how bad discrimination was. Nothing really changed, except they hired a few tokens. Langston was one of them.

He worked three weeks, then they laid him off. A week later, the telephone rang at six o'clock in the morning, telling him things picked back up. It takes thirty days of consecutive work to get into the union.

This has happened to him four times in the past six months. He'd worked five days tearing down an old hospital. Then for three days he removed trash and bricks where a park was supposed to be built. And in the dead of winter, he dug up sewage in the streets for two weeks, down there in a cold hole with wild rats. He'd come in the house so cold his Black lips were white and chapped. His hands were hard and he'd gotten frostbite in his fingertips. Even though he wore four pair of socks in those steel-toed boots, his feet felt like bricks when he took them off in the hallway. The insides were caked with frozen dirt an inch thick and sometimes he was wet. He didn't complain because he was happy to have something to do all day.

Up until recently, Langston mostly worked inside. He put in walls and floors and ceilings, and occasionally did some roof work. He could tear off your roof or slap on a new one, didn't matter to him. But painting is his real love. Said he loves the solitude of being in a big old vacant building with all the windows wide open, his boom box blasting, dipping his stick down into the bucket, and stirring the swirls of fresh thick paint he mixed himself until the sloshiness gets so smooth and creamy that when he strokes the brush against the wall, his big hands just glide. Said he feels like an artist, especially if he's done the Sheetrocking and taping himself.

At home, he works with wood. Sculpts old tree stumps into naked women with strong behinds and delicate upright breasts, chisels the heads of men who could pass for kings or emperors, and builds furniture with legs that don't squeak and drawers that don't stick.

When Christmas approached, Langston had worked a grand total of six days. It was freezing outside and construction work was still drying up. I bought us a six-foot Christmas tree and pretended like I really had the holiday spirit. I got him a membership to a health spa and he got me a red jogging suit. I spent the rent money and said "fuck it," it was Christmas. We got drunk on Scotch and made long-distance telephone calls to our families, made sloppy love, and the next morning got drunk all over again.

New Year's wasn't anything special cause Langston said he didn't have nothing to wear to any of the parties we'd been invited to, and besides, he wasn't in the mood. We stayed home and played backgammon, gin rummy, spades, hearts, casino, and watched the ball drop in Times Square on TV. He'd been down to A Dream Deferred every single morning for the past month, and all he got was a lottery number that moved him up one notch closer to a job. Before him were at least sixty or seventy men who had kids to feed; men who had been out of work much longer than Langston, men who had offered him as much as a dime for one of his Newports, men who used their last dollar to chip in on a pint of rum to keep warm as they stood single file outside the front door of A Dream.

Langston jumped out of bed every morning at five o'clock even though the doors didn't open until seven and it was only a fifteen-minute walk from our apartment. He searched the sock bag until he found just the right ones. Then he laid them at the foot of the bed. He pulled out every thermal undershirt until he found the color he wanted. He tried on different work pants as if he were going to meet my mother for the first time. Then it was which plaid shirt: the one with the split elbow or missing button.

He shaved in slow motion, using the razor to graze his mustache until it was perfect. He made thick Wheatena and filled his thermos with steaming black coffee. By the time I got home at five-thirty, he'd be sitting on the couch with his wool hat still on, his boots mud free, and be sipping his umpteenth cup of coffee and reading the sports section. He read the paper from back to front because he always wanted to know the good news first. I poured myself a large glass of wine and sat next to him on the couch. When I put my arms around him, he inched away from me. I gulped down my wine in silence, and poured myself another glass.

"I don't want no pity from you," he said, "so please, spare me the sympathy would you?"

"Why don't you go to the health spa then, baby."

"For what? I ain't done nothing, so what's the point in working up a sweat?" He'd puff through five or six more Newports and pull out a pint of rum from beneath the couch and pour it in his coffee cup. I edged my way over to the sink and started dinner and was grateful if the telephone rang so I would have somebody nice to talk to.

I tried hard these past few months not to let myself forget that we were so in love that we could hardly keep our clothes on and our hands off each other. When I couldn't get his smell out of my nostrils or his scent off my body and didn't want to. I embarrassed myself many a day walking around sniffing my own wrists and shoulders, trying to get another whiff of him. Sometimes, during dictation, my mind would wander out over a skyscraper and there his face would be, filtering through a moving cloud.

His skin was so smooth it looked like black ice. I could see the muscles in his long arms squeezing me like suctions. Could see his feet dangling over the end of the bed, and gliding up and down my legs. I got tingles all through my body and goosebumps up and down my arms just thinking about how mushy he made me feel. Then the sound of his voice would come out of my boss's lips, and I'd start to giggle. Mr. Huff would look up over his horn-rimmed glasses and say, "You think that's funny, huh, Lola?" I'd snap out of it and sit up straight, direct my eyes toward my fingers, and try to concentrate on what I was getting paid for.

By the end of March we were both evening alcoholics. Every morning I threw out an empty bottle of Chablis or rum. Drinking was the only thing that we shared these days. It was about the only thing we could do to pretend that we weren't depressed. Langston wasn't so eager to get up in the morning and would lay there until I reached over and turned off the alarm and shook him back and forth. "Give me a break," he yelled when I shook him too hard. He rolled back over and pushed his face deeper into the pillow. He stopped shaving except twice a week, but it didn't bother me because I never got close enough to him anymore to feel the new growth scratching my face.

I came home from a poetry reading about nine o'clock. There was a yellow piece of paper Scotch-taped to the door. It was an eviction notice. We had gotten three months behind. I was spending all my money on food and bills and all the things I knew would be most likely to be turned off or taken away. I snatched it from the door. "Umph," he said, when I showed it to him. "What took you so long getting home? It's late." I shook my head at him without saying a word and went to bed thinking that this isn't the man I married. And I don't like this one.

When he came in the room, he grabbed an extra blanket from the linen closet and threw it on the floor. He pulled his pillow off the bed and dropped it on top of it. When he took off his clothes I heard the weight of his body hit the wooden floor through the blanket. He tossed and turned for about ten minutes. It was hard to sleep without him next to me. "Why you sleeping on the floor, Langston?" I asked, sitting up in the dark. "Cause my back hurts," he said, turning his back to me to face the black vinyl trunk. Our mattress is a Posturepedic.

I collapsed into my pillow and stared into the darkness. The mattress was cold. It had been almost a month since we had made love. I leaned over the edge of the bed to stroke his long back. He pushed my hand away. "I don't want no charity." I pulled myself up, turned toward the wall, and listened to him striking matches. I smelled sulfur, then the room filling up with smoke, and heard him sipping his drink. The floor creaked when he turned every few minutes. He inhaled and exhaled six times before I fell asleep.

"Flirting with the men in the liquor store now, huh?"

"What are you talking about, Langston?"

"You know what I'm talking about. Don't play games with me, Lola. I've been watching the way you look at the tall one and when I went in today he told me to tell you hello. And you seem to be getting rather friendly with the old man downstairs too. What's on your mind, huh?"

"You must be going crazy with boredom, Langston, because I'm not flirting with anybody."

"Yeah, well, when I moved in here everybody warned me that you were pretty loose until you met me, that you came and went at all hours of the night and different men were running in and out of here. I should've listened to them. You're nothing but a whore in disguise."

·   ·   ·

After that night, I started calling my girlfriends again because me and Langston were barely speaking. It seemed like every time I was talking on the phone, he would walk in.

"Talking to your lonely girlfriends again? Why don't you go on over and screw one of them since you miss them so much."

Johnny Carson had just finished his monologue, and Langston was laying on the floor with his clean work clothes and hat still on. He was sipping rum from a honey jar.

"You know, Lola, can you understand how useless I feel being in here all day?"

"I'm trying to, Langston, but you aren't making it easy. Every time I try to comfort you, you think I'm feeling sorry for you. I'm damned if I do, and damned if I don't."

"But I feel like I'm being used."

"What the hell do you mean, being used? If anybody should feel used around here it's me. I'm the one who has to sit and smile all day and type, type, type, and come home to see your long face, watching you feel sorry for yourself."

"That's really the only thing you do see too. But I'm here when you come home from your little poetry readings, and you expect me to stand around while you gossip with your lonely little girlfriends. And what do I get for dinner two days in a row? Chinese food. And when was the last time you made love to me? Huh? I have to beg for it and then the only time you want to do it is when you want to. If I was working, if I was making some money, I betcha you'd cook like you used to and I bet you'd want to screw me more often, wouldn't you? Admit it."

"Let me tell you one thing, buster. You're right! I mean look at this whole thing, it's lopsided. You expect me to work, pay all the bills, cook, clean, and screw! Don't you think I get tired? I can't do everything. You married a woman not a damn machine!"

"Yeah, well, you weren't talking like this when we first got married. You couldn't do enough for me, couldn't make love to me enough. But I'll tell you something, I might have to get you some help."

"Good, cause she can sleep on the goddamn floor with you!"

I got this outfit I wear sometimes. I call it my Annie Hall look. It's a snakeskin tie, a brown silk shirt, and some baggy navy blue men's gabardine pants. I wear em with my lizard cowboy boots. I was about to leave for work and Langston was sitting on the couch with a white towel wrapped around him, twisted into a knot at his waist. He had just showered and was letting himself drip dry, all over the floor. I didn't say a word cause it would only start another fight.

"Oh, so the man in the house is going to work," he said.

"Why do you have to say things like that to me, Langston?"

"Well, you're wearing the pants, the tie, and the boots."

"I like this outfit. I was wearing it before I met you and I'm not going to stop now just because your little ego is shattered."

"I never see you wearing a dress anymore, what's wrong, getting your genes mixed up?"

"Maybe if I had somebody to take me to dinner, or a few other decent places, I'd wear a dress!" At this point I wanted to spit in his face for making me feel like I was doing something wrong. I slammed the door in his face.

He opened the door for me when I got home and I could see red rage in his eyes. He was drunk and the rum fumes smelled sour. Before I could put my purse down he grabbed me by the throat and pushed me up against the wall.

"Don't you ever slam the door in my face again. You understand me?"

"Yes, Langston," I said quietly, trying not to ignite him any more than he already was.

"And don't you ever scream at me again, you understand me? I don't raise my voice at you, do I? What are you trying to do, make me feel like a child, like some fool?" He was choking me, and I couldn't breathe. I just looked at him the way my mama used to look at my daddy when he was about to hit her.

"Did you hear me?" he asked in a low voice. Then I felt my right cheek burning from the palm of his huge Black hand. I went numb until I felt the warm blood drip out of my nose. I wanted to kick him but I knew if I did it would be a perfect excuse for him to go crazy on me.

I ran into the bathroom and locked the door. I looked into the mirror and saw the red imprint of his long fingers spread across the right side of my face. I put a cold rag on my forehead and held my head back to stop my nose from bleeding. I hated him. I hated him taking his anger out on me. And most of all I hated him because he was poor.

I opened the bathroom door and walked over to the couch. I sat down. He was sitting in the rocking chair right next to me, smoking a Newport. He was blowing out hard smoke. His bottle of rum was over on the counter and he sipped on hot coffee.

"I'm sorry, Lola, really I am. I didn't mean to do what I did, really," he said, reaching for my arm, but I jerked away like he had just scalded me.

"Don't touch me," I said as I took baby steps toward the sink and poured myself a tumbler of rum. I sat back down on the couch. My face was throbbing. My body trembled as if I were freezing. I walked toward the closet and got my jacket slowly.

"Where you going?" he asked.

"To the store."

"For what?"

"I need some cigarettes," I said.

"Would you get me a pack too, please?" he asked, holding out a dollar bill.

I took his money.

Once outside, I walked slower than I ever have in my life. It was dark and when I exhaled, I could see my white breath flowing and disappearing. When I reached the store, I stood at the counter for a few minutes because I couldn't remember what I had come to buy. On the way back, I opened my pack and lit one. I decided I would write a check and catch a plane to San Francisco. I would call my old boyfriend and he'd pick me up at the airport. I'd wait until Langston was so drunk that he'd fall asleep and be unconscious. By the time I reached the top step, I knew that leaving Langston wouldn't solve our problem.

When I walked back into the living room, he was sitting on the couch, hidden behind a film of white smoke. The floral pillows were squashed and lay sideways against his arm. The pictures above his head looked like framed dead clowns. His fingerprints were smeared around the base of the glass in his hand. I walked toward the kitchen area. The refrigerator looked gray as I leaned my forehead against it. I rolled my head from side to side until my temples tingled from the cold porcelain. For a moment I felt refreshed. But when I swirled around, the golden cracks in the wooden floor seemed to stretch for miles down the hallway.

"Langston, I can't take this shit anymore."

"What shit are you talking about?" He tossed a pillow to the side and got up to get the bottle. He brushed up against me and I didn't move away.

"You know exactly what I'm talking about. You've turned into a real jerk since you've been out of work, and you're taking all your anger out on me when I'm not the one who laid you off."

"I know that." He rushed back toward the couch and then walked to the window. He didn't look outside, he looked at his hands, then clapped them. "Let's go see *Rocky III,* do something to get out of this house. We need a change of pace."

We stopped at the liquor store on the way to buy some more rum. Langston rolled his eyes at all three men behind the counter. We sipped from the bottle like two drunks all the way to the theater. We didn't talk. Fifteen minutes after the movie started, I felt his head drop on my shoulder and his mouth was open. He snored so loud that the people around us stared at me as if he were my child I couldn't control. I shook him a little and he squirmed in the burlap seat. He pushed his torso even further over the armrest until he was nestled under me like he used to be in our bed at night. His aftershave lotion smelled so clean. I stroked my face against the black waves in his hair. I wrapped my arms around him like he was my baby and stroked his arms. I could barely see the screen over his head, but he felt so warm in the dark that I kept rubbing my face against his, feeling his whiskers scratching me and I didn't care. Me and Langston hadn't been this close since Christmas.

When he woke up the credits were rolling. On the way home he said he didn't like the movie because it was phony.

"You didn't even see it, Langston, how can you say that?"

"I saw enough of it to realize that the white boy was gonna come out ahead, again. It always turns out the same way, doesn't it?"

"Well, you're the one who wanted to see the stupid movie in the first place."

"I just wanted to get out of the house."

"So, we're out of the house."

I put on my yellow flannel nightgown and got into bed. It was past midnight and I was so tired my body felt like it was deflating.

Langston made himself a liverwurst sandwich and poured himself another drink. He came into the bedroom and sat the glass on the table near the head of the bed. He unbuttoned his shirt and threw it on the trunk. Then he unzipped his pants and where they fell is where he left them. To my surprise he bent down and kissed me on the cheek and slid under the covers next to me.

"Langston, I'm really tired."

"I'm not interested in making love just because I'm not sleeping on the floor. Sex is the furthest thing from my mind." My eyes closed as if someone were underneath pulling them down like a shade. His ice cubes clinked as he took another long sip. Then I felt his large hand slide up my thigh to my hip.

"Langston, please don't."

"But, baby, I need you," he said. He sounded desperate, and spoke in an ugly, uncaring tone.

"I thought you weren't interested," I said. He acted as if I weren't even there, as if he'd been hypnotized to do this. He climbed on top of me and I tried to push him off but I couldn't, and when he refused to budge, I pinched him on the shoulder as hard as I could. I don't think he even felt it because he didn't stop.

"Leave me alone!" I screamed, forgetting completely about his earlier threats. He jerked away, rolled over to his side of the bed like his feelings were hurt, and guzzled the rest of his rum. He lit a cigarette and watched the fire burn down on the match until it almost reached his fingertips. I curled up into a tight fetal position and moved as close to the edge of the bed as possible. Ten minutes passed. I prayed he would fall asleep, but I heard him crush out his cigarette in the ashtray. The minute hand on the clock didn't seem to move. Finally, ten more minutes passed. If I weren't so tired and he weren't so disgustingly drunk, I could probably get in the mood. I cracked my left eye open, and could see his shadow, a long black mountain against the white wall. Then it moved. I didn't. His breathing grew slow and regulated, and I thought he had surely fallen asleep. But just as I dozed off, I felt my body flipping over. He threw the comforter to the floor and snatched my panties off.

"Lola, I need you so bad, you just don't know how bad." I didn't feel like fighting him. He began slowly, even though he knew I had no intention of moving. He didn't touch me anywhere except there. He never even looked at me; he was in his own world, and I lay there like a car that wouldn't start, feeling like a dead engine. Cold tears ran down my face. I couldn't wipe them away because he was holding my arms against the mattress.

I dried up inside and he worked harder to loosen me up. From one moment to the next I tried to pretend that he had just kissed me softly on my forehead, behind my ear, and that his hairy chest was pressed gently against me. I wished he would stroke my hair, but when I looked up, he was looking at me like I was an alien.

His body collapsed and he kissed me so hard that my lips hurt. His breath tasted like rum and smoke and liverwurst and he was soaking wet. My entire body was slippery, but my forehead was dry. I turned my head quickly to the side so his mouth pressed against my cheek. He didn't even notice. Then I felt his strong tongue twirling over my shoulders, my neck, and inside my ears. When he whispered, "Thank you, baby," in my ear, I thought he was finished. "I'll try harder, baby. I'll find work. I'll do anything, I promise, baby, have faith in me. I love you, baby."

"Take it easy, please, Langston," was all I could say.

"I'm sorry, baby," he said, apologetically. He begged me to move for him, and when I did, within a few minutes it was over. He kissed me, but this time it was warm and soft. I turned on my stomach and felt his warm chest and the rest of his body melt over mine like a mold. He slid his warm arms around me and cupped my breasts in each hand. He felt so good, so warm that now I didn't want him to move.

He got up before me and turned off the alarm clock. He had already showered and shaved because I heard him in the bathroom. I smelled fresh perked coffee. When he came into the bedroom I hid my face under the covers. I didn't know what to say to him. He pulled the covers away and sat down on the bed. He was dressed for work.

"Good morning, baby," he said, bending down to kiss me. I turned my head away. "Good morning, baaaby," he said again.

I pushed him out of my way and jumped out of bed. He looked at me as though he didn't remember. He followed me.

"What's wrong, Lola?"

"I just want you to know that this'll be the last time you ever do what you did to me last night. I don't need to sleep with my own husband if I can't say no without feeling like I'm gonna get raped. How would you feel if the tables were turned, huh?" I poured myself a cup of coffee.

"I'm sorry, Lola, I was drunk, that's all."

"Yeah, drunk. You've got an excuse for everything. What if it was you who had to get up at the crack of dawn and go to work, huh? You want to know something, I bet all these mornings you roam the street and don't even look for work. And I bet you just sit in here all day like a bum. You like watching me act like your slave, like some prostitute taking care of her pimp, don't you?"

I moved away from him, and spilled half-and-half all over the counter, but I ignored it. I wasn't looking at him, didn't even see him. He could've been in another room and I'd have never known it.

"And you want to know something else? If you'd have finished high school, maybe you'd be able to do something else besides pick up and throw bricks and paint dilapidated tenements

for slumlords! What if it was me tearing off your briefs, or slapping you across the face till your nose bled, because I couldn't
find a job?"

My hands and body shook like I was being electrocuted.
Without realizing it, I threw my cup against the door and hot
coffee splattered all over the floor like an oil slick. When I looked
at Langston, his eyes were red and wet. He put on his hat and
coat and turned slowly away from me. The room grew full of a
loud gray silence. He walked out the door, forgetting his Newports and never touching his coffee.

All day long I worried whether or not he would be home
when I got there. I didn't mean to hurt him. Didn't want to
chisel him down to nothing. I just wanted him to know I was
tired of him treating me like shit. By lunchtime, Mr. Huff noticed that I wasn't my cheery self, and asked me if there was
anything wrong. I told him no. He didn't believe me, and insisted that I take the afternoon off.

When I got home, Langston wasn't there. I ran to the bedroom closet and his clothes were still there. I walked back toward
the kitchen. There were no dirty dishes in the sink and he had
cleaned up my mess. The floors shined like gold. The entire
apartment looked like it had been spring-cleaned. The grocery
cart was in front of the couch, full of clean laundry that he'd even
folded. Langston never folds the clothes when he washes.

I was about to take them out of the cart when he walked in
the door. He had a large white bag in his hand. I thought it was
a bottle of rum. Then I smelled the rose.

Released in the winter 1987 edition of *Callaloo*, "Ma'Dear" shows McMillan writing to understand someone else's perspective by centering the kind of character who is too often voiceless. The authentic and unapologetic tone that McMillan will become known for is apparent. The story was dedicated to Estelle Ragsdale, an elder who let McMillan stay in her Queens home when she first arrived in New York City. McMillan recalled that Ragsdale made her laugh and that she told her that she was living her dream: being Black and female and going to college.

Ma'Dear
(for Estelle Ragsdale)

[1987]

Last year the cost of living crunched me and I got tired of begging from Peter to pay Paul, so I took in three roomers. Two of em is live-in nurses and only come around here on weekends. Even then they don't talk to me much, except when they hand me their money orders. One is from Trinidad and the other is from Jamaica. Every winter they quit their jobs, fill up two and three barrels with I don't know what, ship em home, and follow behind on an airplane. They come back in the spring and start all over. Then there's the little college girl, Juanita, who claims she's going for architecture. Seem like to me that was always men's work, but I don't say nothing. She grown.

I'm seventy-two. Been a widow for the past thirty-two years. Weren't like I asked for all this solitude, just that couldn't nobody else take Jessie's place is all. He knew it. And I knew it. He fell and hit his head real bad on the tracks going to fetch us some fresh-picked corn and okra for me to make us some succotash, and never come to. I couldn't picture myself with no other man, even though I looked after years of being alone in this big old house, walking from room to room with nobody to talk to, cook or clean for, and not much company either.

I missed him for the longest time, and thought I could find a man just like him, sincerely like him, but I couldn't. Went out for a spell with Esther Davis's ex-husband, Whimpy, but he was crazy. Drank too much bootleg and then started memorializing on World War I and how hard he fought and didn't get no respect and not a ounce of recognition for his heroic deeds. The only war Whimpy been in is with me for not keeping him around. He bragged something fearless about how he coulda been the heavyweight champion of the world. Didn't weigh but 160 pounds and shorter than me.

Chester Rutledge almost worked ceptin he was boring, never had nothing on his mind worth talking about; claimed he didn't think about nothing besides me. Said his mind was always clear and visible. He just moved around like a zombie and worked hard at the cement foundry. Insisted on giving me his paychecks, which I kindly took for a while, but when I didn't want to be bothered no more, I stopped taking his money. He got on my nerves too bad so I had to tell him I'd rather have a man with no money and a busy mind, least I'd know he's active somewheres. His feelings was hurt bad and he cussed me out, but we still friends to this very day. He in the home, you know, and I visits him regular. Takes him magazines and cuts out his horoscope and the comic strips from the newspaper and lets him read em in correct order.

Big Bill Ronsonville tried to convince me that I shoulda married him instead of Jessie but he couldn't make me a believer of it. All he wanted to do was put his big rusty hands all on me without asking and smile at me with that big gold tooth sparkling and glittering in my face and tell me how lavish I was, lavish being a new word he just learnt. He kept wanting to take me for night rides way out in the country, out there by Smith Creek where ain't nothing but deep black ditches, giant mosquitoes, loud crickets, lightning bugs, and loose pigs, and turn off his motor. His breath stank like whiskey though he claimed and swore on the Bible he didn't drank no liquor. Aside from that his hands were way too heavy and hard, hurt me, sometimes left red marks on me like I been sucked on. I told him finally that I was too light for him, that I needed a smaller, more gentle man and he knew exactly what I meant.

If you want to know the truth, after him I didn't think much about men the way I used to. Lost track of the ones who upped and died or the ones who couldn't do nothing if they was alive no how. So, since nobody else seemed to be able to wear Jessie's shoes, I just stuck to myself all these years.

My life ain't so bad now cause I'm used to being alone, and takes good care of myself. Occasionally I still has a good time. I goes to the park and sits for hours in good weather; watch folks move and listen in on confidential conversations. I add up numbers on license plates to keep my mind alert unless they pass too fast. This gives me a clear idea of how many folks is visiting from out of town. I can about guess the color of every state now too. Once or twice a month I go to the matinee on Wednesdays, providing ain't no long line of senior citizens cause they can be so slow; miss half the picture show waiting for them to count their change and get their popcorn.

Sometimes, when I'm sitting in the park, I feed the pigeons

old cornbread crumbs, and I wonders what it'll be like not looking at the snow falling from the sky, not seeing the leaves form
on the trees, not hearing no car engines, no sirens, no babies
crying, not brushing my hair at night, drinking my Lipton tea
and not being able to go to bed early.

But right now, to tell you the truth, it don't bother me all that
much. What is bothering me is my caseworker. She supposed to
pay me a visit tomorrow because my nosey neighbor, Clarabelle,
saw two big trucks outside, one come right after the other, and
she wondered what I was getting so new and so big that I needed
trucks. My mama used to tell me that sometimes you can't see for
looking. Clarabelle's had it out to do me in ever since last spring
when I had the siding put on the house. I used the last of Jessie's
insurance money cause the roof had been leaking so bad the
wood rotted and the paint chipped so much that it looked like a
wicked old witch lived here. The house looked brand-new, and
she couldn't stand to see an old woman's house looking better
than hers. She know I been had roomers, and now all of a sudden
my caseworker claim she just want to visit to see how I'm doing,
when really what she want to know is what I'm up to. Clarabelle
work in her office.

The truth is my boiler broke and they was here to put in a new
one. We liked froze to death in here for two days. Yeah, I had a
little chump change in the bank, but when they told me it was
gonna cost $2,000 to get some heat I cried. I had $862 in the
bank. $300 of it I had just spent on this couch I got on sale; it was
in the other truck. After twenty years the springs finally broke
and I figured it was time to buy a new one cause I ain't one for
living in poverty, even at my age. $200 was for my church's cross-
country bus trip this summer.

Jessie's sister, Willamae, took out a loan for me to get the
boiler, and I don't know how long it's gonna take me to pay her

back. She only charge me fifteen or twenty dollars a month, depending. I probably be dead by the time it get down to zero.

My bank wouldn't give me the loan for the boiler, but then they keep sending me letters almost every week trying to get me to refinance my house. They must thank I'm senile or something. On they best stationery, they write me. They say I'm up in age and wouldn't I like to take that trip I've been putting off because of no extra money. What trip? They tell me if I refinance my house for more than what I owe, which is about $3,000, that I could have enough money left over to go anywhere. Why would I want to refinance my house at fourteen and a half percent when I'm paying four and a half now? I ain't that stupid. They say dream about clear blue water, palm trees, and orange suns. Last night I dreamt I was doing a backstroke between big blue waves and tipped my straw hat down over my forehead and fell asleep under an umbrella. They made me think about it. And would I do it if I was to die today? They're what got me to thinking about all this dying mess in the first place. It never would've laid in my mind so heavy if they hadn't kept reminding me of it. Who would pay off your house? Wouldn't I feel bad leaving this kind of a burden on my family? What family they talking about? I don't even know where my people is no more.

I ain't gonna lie. It ain't easy being old. But I ain't complaining neither, cause I learned how to stretch my social security check. My roomers pay the house note and I pay the taxes. Oil is sky-high. Medicaid pays my doctor bills. I got a letter what told me to apply for food stamps. That caseworker come here and checked to see if I had a real kitchen. When she saw I had a stove and sink and refrigerator, she didn't like the idea that my house was almost paid for, and just knew I was lying about having roomers. "Are you certain that you reside here alone?" she asked me. "I'm certain," I said. She searched every inch of my cabinets to make sure

I didn't have two of the same kinds of food, which would've been a dead giveaway. I hid it all in the basement inside the washing machine and dryer. Luckily, both of the nurses was in the islands at the time, and Juanita was visiting some boy what live in D.C.

After she come here and caused me so much eruptions, I had to make trip after trip down to that office. They had me filling out all kinds of forms and still held up my stamps. I got tired of answering the same questions over and over and finally told em to keep their old food stamps. I ain't got to beg nobody to eat. I know how to keep myself comfortable and clean and well-fed. I manage to buy my staples and toiletries and once in a while, a few extras, like potato chips, ice cream, and maybe a pork chop.

My mama taught me when I was young that no matter how poor you are, always eat nourishing food and your body will last. Learn to conserve, she said. So I keeps all my empty margarine containers and stores white rice, peas, and carrots (my favorites) or my turnips from the garden in there. I can manage a garden when my arthritis ain't acting up. And water is the key. I drinks plenty of it like the doctor told me and I cheats, eats Oreo cookies and saltines. They fills me right up too. And when I feels like it, rolls homemade biscuits, eats them with Alaga syrup if I can find it at the store, and that sticks with me most of the day.

Long time ago, used to be I'd worry like crazy about gaining weight and my face breaking out from too many sweets, and about cellulite forming all over my hips and thighs. Of course, I was trying to catch Jessie then, though I didn't know it at the time. I was really just being cute, flirting, trying to see if I could get attention. Just so happens I lucked up and got all of his. Caught him like he was a spider and I was the web.

Lord, I'd be trying to look all sassy and prim. Have my hair all did, it be curled tight in rows that I wouldn't comb out for hours till they cooled off after Connie Curtis did it for a dollar and a Budweiser. Would take that dollar out my special savings which I kept hid under the record player in the front room. My hair used to be fine too: long and thick and black, past my shoulders, and mens used to say, "Girl, you sure got a head of hair on them shoulders there, don't it make your neck sweat?" But I didn't never bother answering, just blushed and smiled and kept on walking, trying hard not to switch cause Mama told me my behind was too big for my age and to watch out or I'd be luring grown mens toward me. Humph! I loved it though, made me feel pretty, special, like I had attraction.

Ain't quite the same no more, though. I looks in the mirror at myself and I sees wrinkles, lots of them, and my skin look like it all be trying to run down toward my toes but then it changed its mind and just stayed there, sagging and lagging, laying limp against my thick bones. Shoot, mens used to say how sexy I was with these high cheeks, tell me I looked swollen, like I was pregnant, but it was just me, being all healthy and everything. My teeth was even bright white and straight in a row then. They ain't so bad now, cause ain't none of em mine. But I only been to the dentist twice in my whole life and that was cause on Easter Sunday I was in so much pain he didn't have time to take no X-ray and yanked it right out cause my mama told him to do anything he had to to shut me up. Second time was the last time, and that was cause the whole top row and the fat ones way in the back on the bottom ached me so bad the dentist yanked em all out so I wouldn't have to be bothered no more.

Don't get me wrong, I don't miss being young. I did everything I wanted to do and then some. I loved hard. But you take Jessie's niece, Thelma. She pitiful. Only twenty-six, don't think she made it past the tenth grade, got three children by different men, no husband, and on welfare. Let her tell it, ain't nothing out here but dogs. I know some of these men out here ain't worth a pot to piss in, but all of em ain't dogs. There's gotta be some young Jessies floating somewhere in this world. My mama always told me you gotta have something to give if you want to get something in return. Thelma got long fingernails.

Me, myself, I didn't have no kids. Not cause I didn't want none or couldn't have none, just that Jessie wasn't full and couldn't give me the juices I needed to make babies. I accepted it cause I really wanted him all to myself, even if he couldn't give me no new bloodlines. He was satisfying enough for me, quite satisfying if you don't mind me repeating myself.

I don't understand Thelma, like a lot of these young peoples. I be watching em on the streets and on TV. I be hearing things they be doing to themselves when under the dryer at the beauty shop. (I go to the beauty shop once a month cause it make me feel like thangs ain't over yet. She give me a henna so the silver have a gold tint to it.) I can't afford it, but there ain't too many luxuries I can. I let her put makeup on me too if it's a Saturday and I feel like doing some window shopping. I still know how to flirt and sometimes I get stares too. It feel good to be looked at and admired at my age. I try hard to keep myself up. Every week-day morning at five-thirty I do exercises with the TV set, when it don't hurt to stretch.

But like I was saying, Thelma and these young people don't look healthy, and they spirits is always so low. I watch em on the streets, on the train, when I'm going to doctor. I looks in their eyes and they be red or brown where they supposed to be milky white and got bags deeper and heavier than mine, and I been through some thangs. I hear they be using these drugs of variety and I can't understand why they need to use all these things to get from day to day. From what I do hear, it's supposed to give em much pleasure and make their minds disappear or make em not feel the thangs they supposed to be feeling anyway.

Heck, when I was young, we drank sarsaparilla and couldn't even buy no wine or any kind of liquor in no store. These youngsters ain't but eighteen and twenty, and buys anything with a bite to it. I've seen em sit in front of the store and drank a whole bottle in one sitting. Girls too.

We didn't have no dreams of carrying on like that, and specially on no corner. We was young ladies and young men with respect for ourselfs. And we didn't smoke none of them funny cigarettes all twisted up with no filters that smell like burning dirt. I ask myself, I say Ma'Dear, what's wrong with these kids? They can read, write, and do arithmetic, finish high school, go to college, and get letters behind they names, but every day I hear the neighbors complain that one of they young done dropped out.

Lord, what I wouldn'ta done to finish high school and been able to write a full sentence or even went to college. I reckon I'da been a room decorator. I know they calls it by that fancy name now, interior designer, but it boil down to the same thang. I guess it's cause I loves so to make my surroundings pleasant, even right pretty, so I feels like a invited guest in my own house. And I always did have a flair for color. Folks used to say, "Hazel, for somebody as poor as a church mouse, you got better taste in thangs than them Rockefellers!" Used to sew up a storm too. Covered my mama's raggedy duofold and chairs. Made her a bedspread with matching pillowcases. Didn't mix more than two different patterns either. Make you dizzy.

Wouldn't that be just fine, being an interior designer? Learning the proper names of thangs and recognizing labels in catalogs, giving peoples my business cards wearing a two-piece with white gloves. "Yes, I decorated the Hartleys' and Cunninghams' homes.

It was such a pleasant experience. And they're such lovely people, simply lovely," I'da said. Could'a told those rich folks just what they needed in their bedrooms, front rooms, and specially in the kitchen. So many of em still don't know what to do in there.

But like I was saying before I got all off the track, some of these young people don't appreciate what they got. And they don't know thangs like we used to. We knew about eating fresh vegetables from the garden, growing and picking em ourselves. What going to church was, being honest and faithful. Trusting each other. Leaving our front door open. We knew what it was like to starve and get cheated yearly when our crops didn't add up the way we figured. We suffered together, not separately. These youngsters don't know about suffering for any stretch of time. I hear em on the train complaining cause they can't afford no Club Med, no new record playing albums, cowboy boots, or those Brooke Shields–Calvin Klein blue jeans I see on TV. They be complaining about nonsense. Do they ever read books since they been taught is what I want to know. Do they be learning things and trying to figure out what to do with it?

And these young girls with all this thick makeup caked on their faces, wearing these high heels they can't hardly walk in. Trying to be cute. I used to wear high heels mind you, with silk stockings, but at least I could walk in em. Jessie had a car then. Would pick me up, and I'd walk real careful down the front steps like I just won the Miss America pageant, one step at a time, and slide into his shiny black Ford. All the neighbors peeked through the curtains cause I was sure enough riding in a real automobile with my legitimate boyfriend.

If Jessie was here now I'd have somebody to talk to. Somebody to touch my skin. He'd probably take his fingers and run em through my hair like he used to; kiss me on my nose and tickle me where it made me laugh. I just loved it when he kissed me.

My mind be so light and I felt tickled and precious. Have to sit down sometime just to get hold of myself.

If he was here, I probably woulda beat him in three games of checkers by now and he'd be trying to get even. But since today is Thursday, I'd be standing in that window over there waiting for him to get home from work, and when I got tired or the sun be in my eyes, I'd hear the taps on his wing tips coming up the front porch. Sometime, even now, I watch for him, but I know he ain't coming back. Not that he wouldn't if he could, mind you, cause he always told me I made him feel lightning lighting up his heart.

Don't get me wrong, I got friends, though a heap of em is dead or got tubes coming out of their noses or going all through their bodies every which-a-way. Some in the old folks' home. I thank the Lord I ain't stuck in one of them places. I ain't never gonna get that old. They might as well just bury me standing up if I do. I don't want to be no nuisance to nobody and I can't stand being around a lot of sick people for too long.

I visits Gunther and Chester when I can, and Vivian who I grew up with, but no soon as I walk through them long hallways, I get depressed. They lay there all limp and helpless, staring at the ceiling like they're really looking at something, or sitting stiff in their rocking chairs, pitiful, watching TV, and don't be knowing what they watching half the time. They laugh when ain't nothing funny. They wait for it to get dark so they know it's time to go to sleep. They relatives don't hardly come visit em, just folks like me. Whimpy don't understand a word I say and it makes me grateful I ain't lost no more than I have.

Sometime, we sits on the sunporch rocking like fools; don't say one word to each other for hours. But last time Gunther told me about his grandson what got accepted to Stanford University and another one at a university in Michigan. I asked him where was Stanford and he said he didn't know. "What difference do it make?" he asked. "It's one of those uppity schools for rich smart white people," he said. "The important thang is that my Black grandson won a scholarship there which mean he don't have to pay a dime to go." I told him I know what a scholarship is, I ain't stupid. Gunther said he was gonna be there for at least four years or so, and by that time he would be a professional. "Professional what?" I asked. "Who cares, Ma'Dear, he gonna be a professional at whatever it is he learnt." Vivian started mumbling when she heard us talking, cause she still like to be the center of attention. When she was nineteen, she was Miss Springfield Gardens. Now she can't stand the thought that she old and wrinkled. She started yacking about all the places she'd been to, even described the landscape like she was looking at a photograph. She ain't been but twenty-two miles north of here in her entire life and that's right there in that home.

Like I said, and this is the last time I'm gonna mention it. I don't mind being old, it's just that sometime I don't need all this solitude. You can't do everything by yourself and expect to have as much fun as if somebody was there doing it with you. That's why when I'm feeling jittery or melancholy for long stretches, I read the Bible and it soothes me. I water my morning glories and amaryllis. I babysit for Thelma every now and then, cause she don't trust me with the kids for too long. She mainly call on holidays and my birthday. And she the only one who don't forget my birthday: August nineteenth. She tell me I'm a Leo, that I got fire in my blood. She may be right, cause once in a while I gets a churning desire to be smothered in Jessie's arms again.

Anyway, it's getting late, but I ain't tired. I feel pretty good. That old caseworker thank she gonna get the truth out of me. She don't scare me. It ain't none of her business that I got money coming in here besides my social security check. How they spect a human being to live off $369 a month in this day and age is what I wanna know. Every time I walk out my front door it cost me at least two dollars. I bet she making thousands and got credit cards galore. Probably got a summer house on the Island and goes to Florida every January. If she found out how much I was getting from my roomers, the government would make me pay back a dollar for every two I made. I best to get my tail on upstairs and clear everything off their bureaus. I can hide all the nurses' stuff in the attic; they won't be back till next month. Juanita been living out of trunks since she got here, so if the woman ask what's in em, I'll tell her, old sheets and pillowcases and memories.

On second thought, I thank I'm gonna take me a bubble bath first, and dust my chest with talcum powder, then I'll make myself a hot cup of Lipton's and paint my fingernails clear cause my hands feel pretty steady. I can get up at five and do all that other mess; caseworker is always late anyway. After she leave, if it ain't snowing too bad, I'll go to the museum and look at the new paintings in the left wing. By the time she get here, I gotta make out like I'm a lonely old widow stuck in a big old house just sitting here waiting to die.

McMillan's focus on the things happening around her is front and center in "Quilting on the Rebound." Written in the early 1980s, it was published in 1991 in the anthology *Voices Louder than Words: A Second Collection* when McMillan was teaching at the University of Arizona. The situations that the characters face are still relevant today. The main character tackles the impossible choices facing women now and then: expectations around motherhood, career, romance, and not losing yourself in the process.

Quilting on the Rebound

[1991]

Five years ago, I did something I swore I'd never do—went out with someone I worked with. We worked for a large insurance company in L.A. Richard was a senior examiner and I was a chief underwriter. The first year, we kept it a secret, and not because we were afraid of jeopardizing our jobs. Richard was twenty-six and I was thirty-four. By the second year, everybody knew it anyway and nobody seemed to care. We'd been going out for three years when I realized that this relationship was going no-where. I probably could've dated him for the rest of my life and he'd have been satisfied. Richard had had a long reputation for being a Don Juan of sorts, until he met me. I cooled his heels. His name was also rather ironic, because he looked like a Black Richard Gere. The fact that I was older than he was made him feel powerful in a sense, and he believed that he could do for me what men my own age apparently couldn't. But that wasn't true. He was a challenge. I wanted to see if I could make his head and heart turn 360 degrees, and I did. I blew his young mind in bed, but he also charmed me into loving him until I didn't care how old he was.

Richard thought I was exotic because I have slanted eyes, high cheekbones, and full lips. Even though my mother is Japanese and my dad is Black, I inherited most of his traits. My complexion is dark, my hair is nappy, and I'm five-six. I explained to Richard that I was proud of both of my heritages, but he has insisted on thinking of me as being mostly Japanese. Why, I don't know. I grew up in a Black neighborhood in L.A., went to Dorsey High School—which was predominantly Black, Asian, and Hispanic— and most of my friends are Black. I've never even considered going out with anyone other than Black men.

My mother, I'm glad to say, is not the stereotypical passive Japanese wife either. She's been the head nurse in Kaiser's cardiovascular unit for over twenty years, and my dad has his own landscaping business, even though he should've retired years ago. My mother liked Richard and his age didn't bother her, but she believed that if a man loved you he should marry you. Simple as that. On the other hand, my dad didn't care who I married just as long as it was soon. I'll be the first to admit that I was a spoiled-rotten brat because my mother had had three miscarriages before she finally had me and I was used to getting everything I wanted. Richard was no exception. "Give him the ultimatum," my mother had said, if he didn't propose by my thirty-eighth birthday.

But I didn't have to. I got pregnant.

We were having dinner at an Italian restaurant when I told him. "You want to get married, don't you?" he'd said.

"Do you?" I asked.

He was picking through his salad and then he jabbed his fork into a tomato. "Why not, we were headed in that direction anyway, weren't we?" He did not eat his tomato but laid his fork down on the side of the plate.

I swallowed a spoonful of my clam chowder, then asked, "Were we?"

"You know the answer to that. But hell, now's as good a time as any. We're both making good money, and sometimes all a man needs is a little incentive." He didn't look at me when he said this, and his voice was strained. "Look," he said, "I've had a pretty shitty day, haggling with one of the adjusters, so forgive me if I don't appear to be boiling over with excitement. I am happy about this. Believe me, I am," he said, and picked up a single piece of lettuce with a different fork and put it into his mouth.

My parents were thrilled when I told them, but my mother was nevertheless suspicious. "Funny how this baby pop up, isn't it?" she'd said.

"What do you mean?"

"You know exactly what I mean. I hope baby doesn't backfire."

I ignored what she'd just said. "Will you help me make my dress?" I asked.

"Yes," she said. "But we must hurry."

My parents—who are far from well-off—went all out for this wedding. My mother didn't want anyone to know I was pregnant, and to be honest, I didn't either. The age difference was enough to handle as it was. Close to three hundred people had been invited, and my parents had spent an astronomical amount of money to rent a country club in Marina del Rey. "At your age," my dad had said, "I hope you'll only be doing this once."

Richard's parents insisted on taking care of the caterer and the liquor, and my parents didn't object. I paid for the cake.

About a month before the Big Day, I was meeting Richard at the jeweler because he'd picked out my ring and wanted to make sure I liked it. He was so excited, he sounded like a little boy. It was beautiful, but I told him he didn't have to spend four thousand dollars on my wedding ring. "You're worth it," he'd said, and kissed me on the cheek. When we got to the parking lot, he opened my door and stood there staring at me. "Four more weeks," he said, "and you'll be my wife." He didn't smile when he said it, but closed the door and walked around to the driver's side and got in. He'd driven four whole blocks without saying a word and his knuckles were almost white because of how tight he was holding the steering wheel.

"Is something wrong, Richard?" I asked him.

"What would make you think that?" he said. Then he laid on the horn because someone in front of us hadn't moved and the light had just barely turned green.

"Richard, we don't have to go through with this, you know."

"I know we don't have to, but it's the right thing to do, and I'm going to do it. So don't worry, we'll be happy."

But I was worried.

I'd been doing some shopping at the Beverly Center when I started getting these stomach cramps while I was going up the escalator, so I decided to sit down. I walked over to one of the little outside cafés and I felt something lock inside my stomach, so I pulled out a chair. Moments later my skirt felt like it was wet. I got up and looked at the chair and saw a small red puddle. I sat back down and started crying. I didn't know what to do. Then a punkish-looking girl came over and asked if I was okay. "I'm pregnant, and I've just bled all over this chair," I said.

"Can I do something for you? Do you want me to call an

ambulance?" She was popping chewing gum and I wanted to snatch it out of her mouth.

By this time at least four other women had gathered around me. The punkish-looking girl told them about my condition. One of the women said, "Look, let's get her to the restroom. She's probably having a miscarriage."

Two of the women helped me up and all four of them formed a circle around me, then slowly led me to the ladies' room. I told them that I wasn't in any pain, but they were still worried. I closed the stall door, pulled down two toilet seat covers, and sat down. I felt as if I had to go, so I pushed. Something plopped out of me and it made a splash. I was afraid to get up but I got up and looked at this large dark mass that looked like liver. I put my hand over my mouth because I knew that was my baby.

"Are you okay in there?"

I went to open my mouth, but the joint in my jawbone clicked and my mouth wouldn't move.

"Are you okay in there, miss?"

I wanted to answer, but I couldn't.

"Miss." I heard her banging on the door.

I felt my mouth loosen. "It's gone," I said. "It's gone."

"Honey, open the door," someone said, but I couldn't move. Then I heard myself say, "I think I need a sanitary pad." I was staring into the toilet when I felt a hand hit my leg. "Here, are you sure you're okay in there?"

"Yes," I said. Then I flushed the toilet with my foot and watched my future disappear. I put the pad on and reached inside my shopping bag, pulled out a Raiders sweatshirt I'd bought for Richard, and tied it around my waist. When I came out, all of the women were waiting for me. "Would you like us to call your husband? Where are you parked? Do you feel light-headed, dizzy?"

"No, I'm fine, really, and thank you so much for your concern. I appreciate it, but I feel okay."

I drove home in a daze and when I opened the door to my condo, I was glad I lived alone. I sat on the couch from one o'clock to four o'clock without moving. When I finally got up, it felt as if I'd only been there for five minutes.

I didn't tell Richard. I didn't tell anybody. I bled for three days before I went to see my doctor. He scolded me because I'd gotten some kind of an infection and had to be prescribed antibiotics, then he sent me to the outpatient clinic, where I had to have a D&C.

Two weeks later, I had a surprise shower and got enough gifts to fill the housewares department at Bullock's. One of my old girlfriends, Gloria, came all the way from Phoenix, and I hadn't seen her in three years. I hardly recognized her, she was as big as a house. "You don't know how lucky you are, girl," she'd said to me. "I wish I could be here for the wedding but Tarik is having his sixteenth birthday party and I am not leaving a bunch of teenagers alone in my house. Besides, I'd probably have a heart attack watching you or anybody else walk down an aisle in white. Come to think of it, I can't even remember the last time I went to a wedding."

"Me either," I said.

"I know you're gonna try to get pregnant in a hurry, right?" she asked, holding out her wrist with the watch on it.

I tried to smile. "I'm going to work on it," I said.

"Well, who knows?" Gloria said, laughing. "Maybe one day you'll be coming to my wedding. We may both be in wheelchairs, but you never know."

"I'll be there," I said.

All Richard said when he saw the gifts was, "What are we going to do with all this stuff? Where are we going to put it?"

"It depends on where we're going to live," I said, which we hadn't even talked about. My condo was big enough and so was his apartment.

"It doesn't matter to me, but I think we should wait a while before buying a house. A house is a big investment, you know. Thirty years." He gave me a quick look.

"Are you getting cold feet?" I blurted out.

"No, I'm not getting cold feet. It's just that in two weeks we're going to be man and wife, and it takes a little getting used to the idea, that's all."

"Are you having doubts about the idea of it?"

"No."

"Are you sure?"

"I'm sure," he said.

I didn't stop bleeding, so I took some vacation time to relax and finish my dress. I worked on it day and night. I had learned to sew making quilts with my mother as a young girl, so I was doing all the beadwork by hand. My mother was spending all her free time at my place trying to make sure everything was happening on schedule. A week before the Big Day I was trying on my gown for the hundredth time when the phone rang. I thought it might be Richard, since he hadn't called me in almost forty-eight hours, and when I finally called him and left a message, he still hadn't returned my call. My father said this was normal.

"Hello," I said.

"I think you should talk to Richard." It was his mother.

"About what?" I asked.

"He's not feeling very well," was all she said.

"What's wrong with him?"

"I don't know for sure. I think it's his stomach."

"Is he sick?"

"I don't know. Call him."

"I did call him but he hasn't returned my call."

"Keep trying," she said.

So I called him at work, but his secretary said he wasn't there. I called him at home and he wasn't there either, so I left another message and for the next three hours I was a wreck, waiting to hear from him. I knew something was wrong.

I gave myself a facial, a manicure, and a pedicure and watched Oprah Winfrey while I waited by the phone. It didn't ring. My mother was downstairs hemming one of the bridesmaids' dresses. I went down to get myself a glass of wine.

"How you feeling, Marilyn Monroe?" she asked.

"What do you mean, how am I feeling? I'm feeling fine."

"All I meant was you awful lucky with no morning sickness or anything, but I must say, hormones changing because you getting awfully irritating."

"I'm sorry, Ma."

"It's okay. I had jitters too."

I went back upstairs and closed my bedroom door, then went into my bathroom. I put the wineglass on the side of the bathtub and decided to take a bubble bath in spite of the bleeding. I must have poured half a bottle of Secret in. The water was too hot but I got in anyway. Call, dammit, call. Just then the phone rang and scared me half to death. I was hyperventilating and couldn't say much except, "Hold on a minute," while I caught my breath.

"Marilyn?" Richard was saying. "Marilyn?" But before I had a chance to answer he blurted out what must have been on his mind all along. "Please don't be mad at me, but I can't do this. I'm not ready. I wanted to do the right thing, but I'm only twenty-nine years old. I've got my whole life ahead of me. I'm not ready to be a father yet. I'm not ready to be anybody's husband either, and I'm scared. Everything is happening too fast. I know you think I'm being a coward, and you're probably right.

But I've been having nightmares, Marilyn. Do you hear me, nightmares about being imprisoned. I haven't been able to sleep through the night. I doze off and wake up dripping wet. And my stomach. It's in knots. Believe me, Marilyn, it's not that I don't love you because I do. It's not that I don't care about the baby, because I do. I just can't do this right now. I can't make this kind of commitment right now. I'm sorry. Marilyn? Marilyn, are you still there?"

I dropped the portable phone in the bathtub and got out.

My mother heard me screaming and came tearing into the room. "What happened?"

I was dripping wet and ripping the pearls off my dress but somehow I managed to tell her.

"He come to his senses," she said. "This happen a lot. He just got cold feet, but give him day or two. He not mean it."

Three days went by and he didn't call. My mother stayed with me and did everything she could to console me, but by that time I'd already flushed the ring down the toilet.

"I hope you don't lose baby behind this," she said.

"I've already lost the baby," I said.

"What?"

"A month ago."

Her mouth was wide open. She found the sofa with her hand and sat down. "Marilyn," she said, and let out an exasperated sigh.

"I couldn't tell anybody."

"Why not tell somebody? Why not me, your mother?"

"Because I was too scared."

"Scared of what?"

"That Richard might change his mind."

"Man love you, dead baby not change his mind."

"I was going to tell him after we got married."

"I not raise you to be dishonest."

"I know."

"No man in the world worth lying about something like this. How could you?"

"I don't know."

"I told you it backfire, didn't I?"

For weeks I couldn't eat or sleep. At first, all I did was think about what was wrong with me. I was too old. For him. No. He didn't care about my age. It was the gap in my teeth, or my slight overbite, from all those years I used to suck my thumb. But he never mentioned anything about it and I was really the only one who seemed to notice. I was flat-chested. I had cellulite. My ass was square instead of round. I wasn't exciting as I used to be in bed. No. I was still good in bed, that much I did know. I couldn't cook. I was a terrible housekeeper. That was it. If you couldn't cook and keep a clean house, what kind of wife would you make?

I had to make myself stop thinking about my infinite flaws, so I started quilting again. I was astonished at how radiant the colors were that I was choosing, how unconventional and wild the patterns were. Without even realizing it, I was fusing Japanese and African motifs and was quite excited by the results. My mother was worried about me, even though I had actually stopped bleeding for two whole weeks. Under the circumstances, she thought that my obsession with quilting was not normal, so she forced me to go to the doctor. He gave me some kind of an antidepressant, which I refused to take. I told him I was not depressed, simply I was hurt. Besides, a pill wasn't any antidote or consolation for heartache.

I began to patronize just about every fabric store in downtown Los Angeles, and while I listened to the humming of my machine, and concentrated on designs that I couldn't believe I was creating, it occurred to me that I wasn't suffering from heartache at all. I actually felt this incredible sense of relief. As if I didn't have to anticipate anything else happening that was outside of my control. And when I did grieve, it was always because I had lost a child, not a future husband.

I also heard my mother all day long on my phone, lying about some tragedy that had happened and apologizing for any inconvenience it may have caused. And I watched her, bent over at the dining room table, writing hundreds of thank-you notes to the people she was returning gifts to. She even signed my name. My father wanted to kill Richard. "He was too young, and he wasn't good enough for you anyway," he said. "This is really a blessing in disguise."

I took a leave of absence from my job because there was no way in hell I could face those people, and the thought of looking at Richard infuriated me. I was not angry at him for not marrying me, I was angry at him for not being honest, for the way he handled it all. He even had the nerve to come over without calling. I had opened the door but wouldn't let him inside. He was nothing but a little pipsqueak. A handsome, five-foot-seven-inch pipsqueak.

"Marilyn, look, we need to talk."

"About what?"

"Us. The baby."

"There is no baby."

"What do you mean, there's no baby?"

"It died."

"You mean you got rid of it?"

"No, I lost it."

"I'm sorry, Marilyn," he said, and put his head down. How touching, I thought. "This is all my fault."

"It's not your fault, Richard."

"Look. Can I come in?"

"For what?"

"I want to talk. I need to talk to you."

"About what?"

"About us."

"Us?"

"Yes, us. I don't want it to be over between us. I just need more time, that's all."

"Time for what?"

"To make sure this is what I want to do."

"Take all the time you need," I said, and slammed the door in his face.

He rang the buzzer again, but I just told him to get lost and leave me alone. I went upstairs and sat at my sewing machine. I turned the light on, then picked up a piece of purple and terracotta cloth. I slid it under the pressure foot and dropped it. I pressed down on the pedal and watched the needle zigzag. The stitches were too loose so I tightened the tension. Richard is going to be the last in a series of mistakes I've made when it comes to picking a man. I've picked the wrong one too many times, like a bad habit that's too hard to break. I haven't had the best of luck when it comes to keeping them either, and to be honest, Richard was the one who lasted the longest.

When I got to the end of the fabric, I pulled the top and bobbin threads together and cut them on the thread cutter. Then I bent down and picked up two different pieces. They were black and purple: I always want what I can't have or what I'm not supposed to have. So what did I do? Created a pattern of choosing men that I knew would be a challenge. Richard's was his age. But the others—all of them from Alex to William—were all afraid of something: namely, committing to one woman. All I wanted to do was seduce them hard enough—emotionally, mentally, and physically—so they wouldn't even be aware that they were committing to anything. I just wanted them to crave me, and no one else but me. I wanted to be their healthiest addiction. But it was a lot harder to do than I thought. What I found out was that men are a hard nut to crack.

But some of them weren't. When I was in my late twenties, early thirties, before I got serious and realized I wanted a long-term relationship—I'd had at least twenty different men fall in love with me, but of course these were the ones I didn't want. They were the ones who after a few dates or one rousing night in bed, ordained themselves my "man" or were too quick to want to marry me, and even some considered me their "property." When it was clear that I was dealing with a different species of man, a hungry element, before I got in too deep, I'd tell them almost immediately that I hoped they wouldn't mind my being bisexual or my being unfaithful because I was in no hurry to settle down with one man, or that I had a tendency of always falling for my man's friends. Could they tolerate that? I even went so far as to tell them that I hoped having herpes wouldn't cause a problem, that I wasn't really all that trustworthy because I was a habitual liar, and that if they wanted the whole truth they should find themselves another woman. I told them that I didn't even think I was good enough for them, and they should do themselves a favor, find a woman who's truly worthy of having such a terrific man.

I had it down to a science, but by the time I met Richard, I was tired of lying and conniving. I was sick of the games. I was whipped, really, and allowed myself to relax and be vulnerable because I knew I was getting old.

When Gloria called to see how my honeymoon went, I told

her the truth about everything. She couldn't believe it. "Well, I thought I'd heard em all, but this one takes the cake. How you holding up?"

"I'm hanging in there."

"This is what makes you want to castrate a man."

"Not really, Gloria."

"I know. But you know what I mean. Some of them have a lot of nerve, I swear they do. But really, Marilyn, how are you feeling for real, baby?"

"I'm getting my period every other week, but I'm quilting again, which is a good sign."

"First of all, take your behind back to that doctor and find out why you're still bleeding like this. And, honey, making quilts is no consolation for a broken heart. It sounds like you could use some R and R. Why don't you come visit me for a few days?"

I looked around my room, which had piles and piles of cloth and half-sewn quilts, from where I'd changed my mind. Hundreds of different-colored threads were all over the carpet, and the satin stitch I was trying out wasn't giving me the effect I thought it would. I could use a break, I thought, I could. "You know what?" I said. "I think I will."

"Good, and bring me one of those tacky quilts. I don't have anything to snuggle up with in the winter, and contrary to popular belief, it does get cold here come December."

I liked Phoenix and Tempe, but I fell in love with Scottsdale. Not only was it beautiful but I couldn't believe how inexpensive it was to live in the entire area, which was all referred to as the Valley. I have to thank Gloria for being such a lifesaver. She took me to her beauty salon and gave me a whole new look. She chopped off my hair, and one of the guys in her shop showed me how to put on my makeup in a way that would further enhance what assets he insisted I had.

We drove to Tucson, to Canyon Ranch for what started out as a simple Spa Renewal Day. But we ended up spending three glorious days and had the works. I had an herbal wrap, where they wrapped my entire body in hot thin linen that had been steamed. Then they rolled me up in flannel blankets and put a cold washcloth on my forehead. I sweated in the dark for a half hour. Gloria didn't do this because she said she was claustrophobic and didn't want to be wrapped up in anything where she couldn't move. I had a deep-muscle and shiatsu massage on two different days. We steamed. We jacuzzied. We both had a mud facial, and then this thing called aromatherapy—where they put distilled essences from flowers and herbs on your face and you look like a different person when they finish. On the last day, we got this Persian Body Polish where they actually buffed our skin with crushed-pearl creams, sprayed us with some kind of herbal spray, then used an electric brush to make us tingle. We had our hands and feet moisturized and put in heated gloves and booties, and by the time we left, we couldn't believe we were the same women.

In Phoenix, Gloria took me to yet another resort, where we listened to live music. We went to see a stupid movie and I actually laughed. Then we went on a two-day shopping spree and I charged whatever I felt like. I even bought her son a pair of eighty-dollar sneakers, and I'd only seen him twice in my life.

I felt like I'd gotten my spirit back, so when I got home, I told my parents I'd had it with the smog, the traffic, the gangs, and L.A. in general. My mother said, "You cannot run from heartache," but I told her I wasn't running from anything. I put my condo on the market, and in less than a month it sold for four times what I paid for it. I moved in with my mother and father, asked for a job transfer for health reasons, and when it came through, three months later, I moved to Scottsdale.

The town house I bought feels like a house. It's twice the size of the one I had and cost less than half of what I originally spent. My complex is pretty standard for Scottsdale. It has two pools and four tennis courts. It also has vaulted ceilings, wall-to-wall carpet, two fireplaces, and a garden bathtub with a Jacuzzi in it. The kitchen has an island in the center and I've got a 180-degree view of Phoenix and mountains. It also has three bedrooms. One I sleep in, one I use for sewing, and the other is for guests.

I made close to forty thousand dollars after I sold my condo, so I sent four to my parents because the money they'd put down for the wedding was nonrefundable. They really couldn't afford that kind of loss. The rest I put in an IRA and CDs until I could figure out something better to do with it.

I hated my new job. I had to accept a lower-level position and less money, which didn't bother me all that much at first. The office, however, was much smaller and full of rednecks who couldn't stand the thought of a Black woman working over them. I was combing the classifieds, looking for a comparable job, but the job market in Phoenix is nothing close to what it is in L.A. But thank God Gloria's got a big mouth. She'd been boasting to all of her clients about my quilts, had even hung the one I'd given her on the wall at the shop, and the next thing I know I'm getting so many orders I couldn't keep up with them. That's when she asked me why didn't I consider opening my own shop? That never would've occurred to me, but what did I have to lose?

She introduced me to Bernadine, a friend of hers who was an accountant. Bernadine in turn introduced me to a good lawyer, and he helped me draw up all the papers. Over the next four months, she helped me devise what turned out to be a strong marketing and advertising plan. I rented an eight-hundred-square-foot space in the same shopping center where Gloria's shop is, and opened Quiltworks, Etc.

It wasn't long before I realized I needed to get some help, so I hired two seamstresses. They took a lot of the strain off of me, and I was able to take some jewelry-making classes and even started selling small pieces in the shop. Gloria gave me this tacky T-shirt for my thirty-ninth birthday, which gave me the idea to experiment with making them. Because I go overboard in everything I do, I went out and spent a fortune on every color of metallic and acrylic fabric paint they made. I bought one hundred 100 percent cotton heavy-duty men's T-shirts and discovered other uses for sponges, plastic, spray bottles, rolling pins, lace, and even old envelopes. I was having a great time because I'd never felt this kind of excitement and gratification doing anything until now.

I'd been living here a year when I found out that Richard had married another woman who worked in our office. I wanted to hate him, but I didn't. I wanted to be angry, but I wasn't. I didn't feel anything toward him, but I sent him a quilt and a wedding card to congratulate him, just because.

To be honest, I've been so busy with my shop, I haven't even thought about men. I don't even miss having sex unless I really just think about it. My libido must be evaporating, because when I do think about it, I just make quilts or jewelry or paint T-shirts and the feeling goes away. Some of my best ideas come at these moments.

Basically, I'm doing everything I can to make Marilyn feel good. And at thirty-nine years old my body needs tightening, so I joined a health club and started working out three to four times a week. Once in a while, I babysit for Bernadine, and it breaks my heart when I think about the fact that I don't have a child of my own. Sometimes, Gloria and I go out to hear some music. I frequent most of the major art galleries, go to just about every football and basketball game at Arizona State, and see at least one movie a week.

I am rarely bored. Which is why I've decided that at this point in my life, I really don't care if I ever get married. I've learned that I don't need a man in order to survive, that a man is nothing but an intrusion, and they require too much energy. I don't think they're worth it. Besides, they have too much power, and from what I've seen, they always seem to abuse it. The one thing I do have is power over my own life. I like it this way, and I'm not about to give it up for something that may not last.

The one thing I do want is to have a baby. Someone I could love who would love me back with no strings attached. But at thirty-nine, I know my days are numbered. I'd be willing to do it alone, if that's the only way I can have one. But right now, my life is almost full. It's fun, it's secure, and it's safe. About the only thing I'm concerned about these days is whether or not it's time to branch out into leather.

Written during the 2020 COVID lockdown and George Floyd uprising, "From Behind the Counter" is the first short story McMillan wrote and published after becoming a bestselling novelist in the early 1990s. It was penned at the request of Pulitzer Prize–winning journalist Nikole Hannah-Jones, creator of *The 1619 Project: A New Origin Story,* an ongoing initiative from *The New York Times* that "speaks directly to our current moment . . . It reveals long glossed-over truths around our nation's founding—and the way that the legacy of slavery did not end with emancipation but continues to shape modern American life." It is a return to McMillan's short-story roots, and a reminder of her mandate to write from the heart in order to understand someone else's perspective. "From Behind the Counter" reminds us that the everyday realities surrounding the civil rights movement are not so different from the reality of life defined by COVID lockdowns and the Black Lives Matter movement.

From Behind the Counter

[2021]

My cousin who lives out in California told me a long time ago that right before an earthquake there was a stillness in the air. He said to watch out because it could mean good news or bad news but it would be something you can't prepare for. Well, I missed work yesterday because the bus broke down and by the time I walked to Woolworth's it woulda almost been time for me to turn around and come on back home so I got a ride to the closest gas station and they let me use their phone but my boss didn't care what the reason was I wasn't coming and docked me the seven dollars I woulda made. It took me almost two hours to walk back home and the whole time I didn't see one leaf move on any of the trees. Even when I turned the corner and walked up the hill, I didn't feel a breeze.

I just hoped this wasn't a sign the baby was coming early. Me and my wife been struggling to get on our feet here in Greensboro after staying with kinfolks a whole year and now with a baby on the way I need every dime I can get, which is why I haul trash to the dump on my off days.

The bus ran fine today and this morning was just like most mornings. I walked out front to clean off the counter. I tried not to watch the parade of mostly white people carrying bags full of everything I couldn't afford. When four young colored men in trench coats walked in through the glass doors, I nodded hello, thinking they must be looking for a job, but before I could guess again each one stopped right below the giant sign that said WHITES ONLY and one by one they sat down at the counter and each one set what looked like a briefcase on the floor next to his legs, which was when I felt all the air in the diner evaporate.

My heart hurt from beating so hard. I thought maybe they might be confused or lost even though they didn't look it. They looked determined. I made myself breathe.

"Y'all look like you can read," I whispered, glancing up at the sign and then into their eyes.

Just then Mary, a waitress nobody liked because she cursed like a sailor, walked down the counter tapping her pencil, which was when the tooth I needed to see a dentist about started beating like it had a heart and it felt like I was about to have an asthma attack even though I don't have asthma.

"Y'all must can't read. But them suits won't help," she said, looking down at the young men. "Y'all still colored."

My forehead was sweating cause I started thinking about the time my cousin got run over by a white woman for smiling at her at a stop sign and she waited for him to step off the curb and take a few steps which was when she pressed on the gas, hit him hard enough we heard his ankle crack. When we told the police and gave them her license plate number, they didn't even bother to write it down.

"Yes, we can read," said the one wearing glasses. He sounded smart. They all looked smart. I wanted to ask them where they worked but they looked too young to have jobs where they would wear what I could see under those trench coats was suits.

"We would like a cup of coffee. Please."

"You know y'all can't sit here."

"We are already sitting here," the one at the end said.

He sounded so proper I wondered if he might be from New York. I was scared. Why'd they have to pick today to do this? I was waiting for my check, and this foolishness might make me lose my job and maybe not get paid. I got a baby just waiting to meet me. Our rent is three days late and my wife had to stop cleaning houses when she couldn't stand the smell of bleach. And nobody can help us because everybody we know is poor.

I heard the cooks talking about how much nerve the niggers had. But they just politely kept asking for a cup of coffee. The waitresses pretended they was deaf.

Finally, one of the young men said, "Our money is just as good as anyone else's."

A different waitress said, "No, it ain't."

But the young men didn't get up. They reached down and pulled out thick books from their satchels and then set them on the counter, opened them right up like they was all studying the same thing. Where did they get this courage from? Was it from those books? I wondered what they was studying and if there was a class they took on bravery and if they knew other brave colored people? One day I wanted to know what courage felt like, too. I was trying to see what they was reading but it was hard to read upside down. I saw numbers. Strange numbers. I saw a black-and-white picture of the world. Another one about science. And history. I wanted to know whose history? But I couldn't ask. I mostly read the Bible.

I prayed all day the police wouldn't walk through the glass doors and try to yank them off those swivel chairs and when them young men resisted—which I could tell they would—that they wouldn't get dragged outside—one by one—then shot and killed for every time they kept on asking for a cup of coffee and didn't get it.

Even when those news people came and turned them bright lights and cameras on, and crowds in all shades came from inside and outside the store, jumping up and down to see what was going on, them young men did not move. They just kept asking for a cup of coffee.

By now, the waitresses was just ignoring them like they weren't even there. I wanted to say something to the young men but I was scared I would get fired. When I picked up the rubber tray full of dirty dishes and walked past them I did push a fork so it would fall on the floor and when I bent down to pick it up I locked eyes with all four of them and they could see I was proud.

I didn't look at any of them again because if something happened to them I didn't want to remember their faces.

I pretended I needed to go to the bathroom and walked through the store into the men's room. I went inside an empty stall, closed the toilet lid, and sat down. I wondered how all this was gon' turn out? I knew it wasn't about coffee, but what would happen if they did get served a cup? Would that mean they could maybe order some eggs and bacon and toast and orange juice and sit there and eat while they read? Me, I never really wanted to sit next to white people to eat. I didn't trust them. But I also never liked that they was the ones who decided it. Just like they was the ones who decided we would be slaves and when we should be free. I always wondered, what made them think they was better than us just because they was—I mean were—white? I decided that when I got home, I was gon' tell my wife we need to start telling each other how we really feel about how we living. We need to stop being scared of white people and stop acting like we ain't free.

When the store was closing, the police ushered the men out the back door. As the door slammed shut, my boss put his plaid jacket on, headed out toward the front door, and said, "See you tomorrow. And don't be late."

I finished cleaning up the kitchen and went out front and started wiping the counter up and down with a damp rag. The icebox was humming and then it just stopped. Silence can be loud is what I was thinking as I sat down on a stool like I owned the place. I swiveled a few times, staring at the stools where the four young men had sat all day, which was when I threw my damp rag on the floor and poured myself a cup of lukewarm coffee and took a long sip, looking at that empty counter, and at the stools, and up at the WHITES ONLY sign, which was when I felt my body rise up and my arms reached up and I pulled it down.

UNPUBLISHED
FICTION

Developed during McMillan's Yaddo residency in 1982, "Can't Close My Eyes to It" is a heartbreaking coming-of-age story told through the first-person perspective of a young woman learning life lessons during visits to her grandmother. It deftly and subtly explores the world of women's relationships to one another, a theme McMillan has explored endlessly over her long career as a novelist. The grandmother in this story could be seen as an early inspiration for Hazel, the seventy-two-year-old main character in "Ma'Dear," and foreshadows the devastating loss of McMillan's own mother a decade later.

Can't Close My Eyes to It

I was there in her living room that day. A little shack on Van Ness Street, the front porch sagging down toward the ground, slats and planks loosened and some missing. Her old fat chair sat to the left, the claw feet stuck in the cracks of rotted wood. I still don't remember what color it was. But it was dull. To the right, behind the chair stood one opaque window dressed in olive-green brocade. It was scary and even then I knew it was depressing. Nobody ever tried to peek into this window to see if Grandma Maybelle was home either, except my mama, when she dropped me off to keep her company, or Miss Elizabeth Cates, who lived right next door. She was old as dirt. And pretended she was really a Black movie star. Her house was supposed to be white but it wasn't. And it leaned too close to Grandma Maybelle's fence. I was afraid of her ugly dogs that foamed at the mouth because they barked at me like I had done something to them.

Miss Elizabeth was also nosey, and peeked through her dark burgundy drapes that looked like the kind you see in a funeral parlor or in church when they dip you in water to baptize you. She enjoyed getting on everybody's nerves and she was good at it. I did not like her. For starters: Because she would not shut up her barking dogs. Because she grinned at everything you said even when she wasn't listening to you. She had a gold tooth on the top right that didn't make her look as glamorous as she thought. Her pancake makeup was so thick it cracked and fell off her face in little specks on whatever dress she was wearing, which was always some kind of crazy print and so tight the hem would creep up but I pretended not to notice although once it got up so high on her thighs I saw the top of her stockings struggling from that little round rubber thing pushing through it that I suppose was meant to hold them up. I never said a word because apparently she couldn't feel the air rising between her thighs since they were closed, or how high her dress had risen. I just did my best to stop myself from laughing.

She always tried to get me to come over to sit with her, to keep her company, but Grandma Maybelle wasn't having it.

"Get your own granddaughter," she told Miss Elizabeth one afternoon I'd been sitting in her kitchen too long. They were neighbors but not friends. Plus, Miss Elizabeth's house smelled like something dead was in it she hadn't thrown out. I also didn't trust her. But my mama told me to always be nice to my elders or I would have a hard time getting into heaven. But how did she know? I wondered if anybody had been and came back to tell her what it was like. No they had not.

Grandma told me not to eat anything when I went over there because Miss Elizabeth had roaches and she didn't want me bringing them back to her house. Mice were enough. But Miss Elizabeth always tried to con me with a nickel to empty her trash when I knew it was worth a dime for my time. She also had about a million cats crawling all over the furniture because Grandma said Miss Elizabeth also had rats and the dogs weren't interested in catching them. I did not like the way her house smelled: like wet fur, and I did not like the sound of purring, especially when one of them jumped up in my lap. I would push them off hard enough for them to realize they should think twice about doing it again. I stopped hearing them purr. They knew I didn't like them and after fifty years, I still don't.

I asked her once: "Miss Elizabeth, where is your husband?"

"What you know about a husband?" she asked me like I wasn't supposed to ask her this kind of question. As if I was being too grown.

"Where'd he go?"

"You tell me," she said. "Because I would sure like to meet him."

I told Grandma what she said, and Grandma said, "Elizabeth lies through her teeth. She was married for five minutes because she wanted to be the husband and the wife and she was too bossy. She just wanted to play house. Plus, it turned out she didn't like to do things most husbands and wives do at least two or three times a month which you don't need to know about right now. But Elizabeth seem to like being miserable and she makes everybody around her miserable which is why she got all those dog-gone cats and those ugly dogs. They her kids."

I did not want to know any more than that. But I did want Grandma to tell me about her husband, who was my grandfather I had never met.

"Where did my grandpa go?" I asked her after I finished drinking a tall glass of orange Kool-Aid I had put too much sugar in. Grandma acted like she didn't hear me but I knew she had. But I repeated my question.

"I don't know. He took a Greyhound to Detroit five years ago and I have not heard a word from him since. Which means he probably dead."

I remember having more questions but I was told as a kid not to ask grown-ups too many questions because some things I wasn't supposed to know. So I didn't.

Grandma was a roly-poly woman and everybody said she used to be pretty when she was young but I thought she was pretty then. I already knew that beauty was subjective. Yes, her cheeks were puffy but her gray eyes were slits that cut into her face and made her look like she had a little Chinese somewhere in her blood. When I grew older, I would wonder just how much of what she'd seen was hiding behind them. Even her taupe skin pushed up against her wide nose on both sides made me wonder if it could be possible. But who cared? I saw so much on her face. And so what if little brown specks were either freckles or age spots spattered from one cheek to the other? Although I was surprised when I discovered that Grandma's teeth weren't hers when I saw her dentures floating in sizzling water in a canning jar. But I never mentioned it.

For the longest time I thought Uncle Coots was her new husband who just happened to live somewhere else because there was nowhere for him to sleep. Grandma slept in a twin bed because there was barely enough room for her dresser. I was the only one allowed to sleep on the couch, which I didn't like because it dipped in the middle and too many behinds had sat on it. Even still, Uncle Coots always seemed to be there. He was a giant who sat on the front porch with Grandma in a chair so close to Miss Elizabeth's he could've tipped into her side yard but nothing was there except a bent-up wire fence that Uncle Coots kept promising to fix for Grandma but never got around to it. He said his back hurt him when he bent over for too long even though he shot a lot of pool down at Sneaky's and he drank a lot of port and his eyes crisscrossed, stared at each other reluctantly, and I wondered how he ever got a ball in the pocket. Grandma always used to say, "Coots, you can't see for looking. That's your real problem."

Apparently, getting glasses never crossed his mind. He would just laugh so hard he would make a squeaking sound that came out the corner of his mouth. Everybody called him Crazy Coots even though he wasn't crazy, he just pretended to be because he liked the attention, but mostly the laughs since it made him feel like a celebrity. He was also not my real uncle and I didn't know why I didn't want to like him. Maybe because he didn't seem to serve a real purpose but waited for things to break or go wrong to give himself something to do. Which I suppose kept him busy. Like when Grandma tried to push a towel through the roller on her washing machine and it got stuck, Uncle Coots slammed his big hand on the lever and the rollers would pop open, leaving the towel unsure where it was supposed to go. He looked for dead mice just to take them out the trap. Hammered or glued stuff or used a screwdriver for a lot of things I never noticed needed attention. But after he did something that pleased Grandma, this was when he would cock his gray Stetson to the side, that Royal Crown pomade leaving a continuous brown stain below the trim all around the brim, and he thought he was so cool because he had served a purpose. Maybe I did like him.

"Put it right here," he would say to Grandma, pointing a long finger toward his cheek, and he would bend down and Grandma would close her eyes and act like she was holding her breath, and then give him a quick peck and push him away like he was a nuisance.

Uncle Coots was as far from handsome as a man could get. I never got too close to him because he didn't smell like he bathed on a regular basis, even though I could see talcum powder hiding in the jungle of gray hairs on his chest.

But Grandma liked him because he was reliable and he was big and husky and he didn't use curse words and after a few shots of Hennessy or Old Crow he seemed to grow and get stronger. He would volunteer to lift or push everything that was too heavy for her before she had a chance to even think about it. Other than that, he didn't do all that much for her except sit on the front porch and yell at or curse people out for no reason that walked by since not many folks had cars back then.

"Hey, Big-Head, don't you owe me some money?"

"You had that shirt on two days in a row. You scared of Tide?"

He would laugh at his own jokes.

I laughed, too, just because I thought I was supposed to.

"Your Uncle Coots get his jokes confused which is why don't nobody but him think they're funny," Grandma would often say just to mess with him.

"You used to think they was funny, May," he said.

"I used to think a lot of things was funny," she said.

Come to think of it, I was a little nosey myself. I liked listening to the things old people talked about. I remember one time I saw him wink at her and she winked back! I saw it with my own eyes. I wondered what that meant. I also remember looking back and forth at them both and did not understand what was going on that would make either of them wink. Which was why I started winking, too. Even at Kevin, a white boy who blew me a kiss after I did it at the water fountain.

He turned red.

.   .   .

"Coots!" Grandma yelled. "Can you run and get me some snuff, and Lil' Bit, could you please empty Grandma's spittoon? I'll give you some of my butterscotch candy."

Grandma was the only one who called me Lil' Bit, which I loved, and she always used candy to bribe me when it wasn't necessary. She didn't have to reward me because I would do anything for her. I liked being in her company. And I loved her voice. It was like a cello. Which was soft even when she raised it.

But I didn't like the way her snuff smelled. Like wet dirt with something sour and sweet in it. What I did know was right after she used her tiny spoon to spread the brown powder inside the dry canal between her gums and her bottom lip, she sucked until that snuff became brown juice and then swallowed it. A few minutes later she always perked up.

One day I asked her if I could try it.

"This is just for old folks," she said.

But once, when she was taking a nap and I was watching Perry Como singing a song I didn't like on TV, I snuck and put some of her snuff on my tongue to see what would happen. I threw up. Grandma woke up and saw my bottom teeth were brown. She slapped my hand and said, "This is what you get for not believing what I told you. Grandma wouldn't lie to you. Now go get that 7-Up out the Frigidaire and swish it around inside your mouth and spit it out until you don't see no color."

Uncle Coots did everything she asked him to. Rubbed her feet when they were swollen, which was every time he came over, but her feet didn't look swollen to me. They were always the same size when she slid them out of her raggedy "house shoes," as she called them. I had never heard the word "slippers" until I spent the night at a white girl's pajama party up on Strawberry

Lane and Kathy Hale asked me: "Where are your slippers, Monica?" I had on white bobby socks. And slept in them in case something happened and one of them tried to kill me.

Coots made up jokes to make her laugh and her huge breasts sometimes fell out through the V of her housedress and she just pulled them up and pushed them over and under her armpits and pressed down. Good brassieres were too expensive.

Miss Elizabeth was jealous of Grandma Maybelle because nobody visited her, and when she waved to folks who passed by when she sat on her wooden swing on the front porch that wouldn't swing when she sat in it, most people didn't wave back because Elizabeth thought she was better than everybody else even though this was the poor part of town and everybody used to say: "She thank her shit don't stink." I heard a lot of people say this but I was too afraid to ask anybody what it meant. But I knew she was a bitch, even at twelve, and she seemed to be proud of being a bitch. She didn't seem to like anybody.

Which didn't stop her from wearing too much lipstick. I supposed she thought it would make her more attractive, but it made her look like a clown because her lips were thick and she put a hard line of lipstick inside them to make them appear to be smaller. But she looked like something scared her. Or like she was just about to go up in flames. I remember her teeth were always red at the bottom from smoking cigarettes and I didn't realize they were dentures until she told me she would pay me a dollar if I cleaned her kitchen and when I went to move a bowl full of water, inside it were her false teeth fighting for space. I was wondering what age would I need dentures and what happened to their real teeth.

I remember thinking that Miss Elizabeth's red wig didn't help her cause, because she'd put pink sponge rollers all around it like it was her hair and she would sometimes sit on her hot cement steps looking through Spiegel catalogs and even folding the corners back when she saw something she liked. She wanted somebody to honk at her but when they did they pressed and pressed and Miss Elizabeth would wave like she was on a float in a parade. I saw them laugh.

But Miss Elizabeth was not cheap, even though she was poor as everybody else who lived in this town, even white folks who lived on the north end were, too, but they pretended not to be as poor as Black people—or colored, as we were called, and even called ourselves back then. Miss Elizabeth also sewed her own clothes, which looked like it, and she often stood on her front porch like she was a model and yelled, "Hey, Maybelle! How you like this?" And she would swirl around and smile.

"It look just like all the rest, Elizabeth. Where you going to wear it with all that cleavage when you don't go no further than that top step or the one leading inside Mt. Olive Baptist Church?"

"You just jealous. But I can make you one," she said.

"No thank you," Grandma said. "I got enough dresses."

Coots, who always seemed to be at Grandma Maybelle's during daylight hours, would hold his head down and squeal so that the saliva made a squishing sound when he did.

This went on for years, and on my thirteenth birthday, Grandma gave me five dollars to go on a shopping spree at Kmart but because Miss Elizabeth hadn't come out of the house for a day, Grandma said, "Go run over and check on her for me, baby." Instead, I just yelled: "MISS ELIZABETH IF YOU'RE HOME OPEN YOUR DRAPES UP PLEASE!"

I was careful not to talk "country," as Mama would say. Me and my two older sisters and brother always had to use contractions and we were not allowed to say "ain't" for any reason whatsoever. Even though I liked saying it.

Grandma took her hairbrush and popped me upside my head

but because my cornrowed braids were so thick, I didn't feel any pain. "What Grandma tell you about yelling like you out in the country? And just do what I ask you to do because one day it could be a fire and I should not have to say it twice. Now run on over there, chile. Something is wrong."

So I did.

When I knocked on the door the dogs started barking like I was breaking in and the cats were meowing like little tigers and Miss Elizabeth didn't answer. Grandma couldn't walk over here because she had just gotten out of the hospital for gallbladder surgery and Uncle Coots was down at the pool hall.

"Go run down to Gabe's and get your Uncle Coots. Tell him something ain't right."

And I did.

But he wasn't there.

And he didn't have a phone wherever it was he lived.

"She's dead. I know she in there dead," Grandma said.

And Grandma was right.

I had never seen a dead person before and was too scared to get the key under her doormat to open the door. I just peeked in through the open inch of her drapes and saw her on the floor. Cats were walking on top of her and I screamed so loud and ran so hard I tripped on her steps and fell on my elbows but I didn't feel the pain until I saw the blood.

Grandma told me she would but then decided not to go to Miss Elizabeth's funeral because she said she was tired of going to funerals and it seemed like there was one every weekend, which made her wonder if she might be next. Uncle Coots took flowers. Plus, Grandma said the truth be told, she never really liked Elizabeth but just tried to be nice because she knew she was lonely in that house since her first husband moved to Canada and married a Canadian woman half his age even though he was married to Miss Elizabeth, and still was to this day.

"I tried to like her but it was just too hard. She liked to gossip too much and keep things going that shoulda been ended."

"I thought she was nice, Grandma," I said, and then thought maybe I shouldn't have.

"That's good. Always trust your own feelings," she said.

Even though I didn't exactly know what she meant by that and it would take years for me to understand.

"She was too nosey," Grandma said, as if she was trying to think of reasons why she shouldn't go to her funeral. "And plus she still owed me sixty-two dollars and I knew she had it after she got that insurance money from when her mama died."

But when I heard Grandma sitting on the back porch steps crying, I knew there were other reasons why she didn't or couldn't go.

I think I was in seventh grade. Grandma had lost a lot of weight and did not look like herself. Uncle Coots had to walk with a cane, and it looked like everything on him was sliding downward. His eyes drooped. He had breasts. His big belly sat in his lap because his suspenders had lost their elasticity. His fingers were crooked because arthritis had decided they were as good a place as any to attack him. Uncle Coots was now weak. He knew it. Grandma knew it. And I knew it, which was why I started running errands for both of them.

I never did know where Coots lived, and sometimes, when I came over to Grandma's, he'd be asleep on the floor, with a brocade pillow under his head, and Grandma had put a flannel blanket over him. Sometimes when I tried to step over him as quietly as I could, he would wake up and not know where he was. But he recognized me.

"Hey, good lookin'," he always said. "Looking just like your mama."

Sometimes when he tried to sit up, he couldn't, and he pretended he could. I held out my hand but he wouldn't take it.

"Could you hand me that broom over there, sweetie?"

And after I did, he said, "Hand me the long end."

"Grandma said when you ask someone to do something for you, you should always say 'please,' Uncle Coots."

This was what I would later learn would be my mantra, just to remind him that good manners would always matter.

"Would you please hand Uncle Coots the broom, Monica?"

And I did, but I knew I had gotten on his nerves because he never called me by my real name. But he took it and pushed it against the couch cushion, which made him inch up enough to come to a sitting position.

"Getting old is not fun," he said. "Take care of yourself and you won't end up like me and your grandma."

By the time he was able to sit upright, canals were running down his sideburns and red forehead past both sides of his round nostrils. I remember running to get him some toilet paper, which he used to dry his face. Grandma did not have dish towels that I can remember. She had rags.

"Read your grandma something, baby," Grandma would always say, but it was really an ask. It didn't matter what it was. Back then I didn't know she couldn't read, she just made me think she needed new glasses.

One day, even though I was scared, I asked her a question I wasn't supposed to ask.

"How old are you, Grandma?"

I was snapping green beans and tossing them into a big navy blue pot with white speckles on it.

"Why you want to know?"

"I was just wondering," I said, as politely as possible.

"Fifty-nine."

"Is that old?"

"Maybe."

"Are you scared to die?" I clearly remember asking.

"No."

"Why not, Grandma?"

"Because when it's your time, it's your time."

"Says who?"

"Watch your tone, now, baby. But God. He calls when he's ready for you."

"What if you just don't answer?"

I remember the way she looked at me. She squinted her eyes like a cat, as if I was getting on her nerves or she didn't have a legitimate answer.

"Can you go in the kitchen and get me a glass of iced tea out the icebox, please, baby?"

"Yes, ma'am," I said, and jumped up too fast and got a splinter in my hand.

"Coots!" Grandma yelled. But he was asleep, leaning against one of the wooden beams that held that side of the roof of the front porch up.

Coots, who was snoring and drooling, jumped up like he didn't know where he was, causing his hat to fall on a patch of grass. "Who called me?"

"I asked you two years ago if you would run and get me some snuff and while you at it, would you pick me up some black licorice, and a bag of skins. Please?"

"With what? My good looks, May?"

"Shut up, Coots," she said, and reached inside her left bra cup and whipped out a five-dollar bill, which made Uncle Coots's eyes open wide and I remember seeing the red veins that looked like freeways, seemed to move.

"Baby girl, you want a pop or something?" she asked.

"No thank you, Grandma."

"What's wrong with you, gal?" Coots asked. "It's free."

"I'm not thirsty or hungry," I said.

"But you might be later," he said, and held out his hand for the bill and sauntered on down the sidewalk that was higher in some spots because the roots from the weeping willow trees were in search of more soil.

"What you wanna be when you grow up?" Grandma asked me out of the blue. I think she was watching one of her favorite TV shows, *Ed Sullivan,* because I think I was getting close to being a teenager at the time—I did not have any sign of breasts or a period, which would take forever. I wouldn't get either one until I was going into my sophomore year.

"I don't know, Grandma."

"I hope you go to college," she said. "You know negroes can go to college and even girls so if you don't wanna grow up poor like most all of us is now, keep getting good grades and figure out something you good at when you get to college and do not let any boys get under your skirt or inside your pants or it will mess up your whole life."

"I won't," I said.

"Promise Grandma you won't."

"I promise."

"And tell all your girl cousins the same thing. All babies is cute but they grow up and then you gots to do everything for em and forget about yourself. Just look at your mama."

I didn't understand exactly what she meant by that but I was too scared to ask her. My mama had four kids and my daddy was a good daddy and he worked at the foundry where they did something with coal because he came home full of soot and he was already Black. Plus he gave Mama his entire paycheck. She cleaned houses for rich white folks who lived on the water. Mama dropped out of high school in tenth grade. But so did most of her friends. What I did know was a lot of my older cousins already had kids and did not finish high school and I never went to any weddings but my mama threatened to kill me if I even thought about having sex before I graduated from high school so Grandma wasn't telling me anything I hadn't already heard before. Plus, the whole idea of sex scared me. And I already knew I did not want to have any kids because I baby-sat enough to know they could get on your nerves without stopping and they took up all your time and I wanted some for myself.

"What do you like to do?" Grandma asked.

"I don't know," I said, because I didn't. I don't think I was thirteen.

"Think of something you like doing."

"Eating."

She cut her eyes at me. And then realized I was kidding. I wanted her to laugh. Something I hadn't seen her do in a long time. Especially after they tore down Miss Elizabeth's house because it was full of termites. Nobody had bought the lot, which made her yard look like a graveyard without graves. People had started turning it into a junkyard. Toilets. Dilapidated sofas. Bedsprings. Doors. I even saw a motorcycle.

"Something you could get paid to do," Grandma said.

"I don't know what you can get paid to do besides cleaning house if you're colored and a girl."

"Don't you ever let me hear you say that as long as I'm alive. Do you hear me?"

"Yes, ma'am," I said, even though I knew what I said was true.

"Times is changing for us. You can find out what you good at and what you want to be when you get to college," she said. "Can you turn it up some, I can't hear Ed."

"What kind of college?" I asked, since Grandma seemed to know more about college than I did.

"I don't know. The kind where you go for four or five years and get a doctrine that says you are somebody."

"But I thought I was already somebody?"

"You are, baby girl, you are. But that doctrine will give you choices. You can be anything you want to be. But you got time. Look in magazines. Look at all the things rich white people do, especially men and not just white women, since most of them stay home or is secretaries. What you want is a good paycheck and respect. Ed is sure not cute, is he?"

I did not like *The Ed Sullivan Show,* even in color, which was how we could watch everything ever since Coots hit the numbers for six hundred dollars—a whole lot of money in those days—and he spent almost all of it on a color TV, which he gave to Grandma as long as she let him watch *Bonanza* and *Adventures in Paradise,* which Grandma even liked because she said one day she'd like to sail anywhere. Uncle Coots even gave me five dollars, which I used to buy a pair of white Keds and white bobby socks so I could make all the white girls sick with envy at my school. We were poor.

This TV was what made me wonder if Coots was really Grandma's boyfriend because he did what most husbands were supposed to do, at least the way Donna Reed's husband did for her—everything. But Coots couldn't have been Grandma's husband. And they were too old to be boyfriend and girlfriend, so I didn't know what his role was back then. Of course I knew all grown-ups had sex, but not old grown-ups like Grandma and Uncle Coots. Just the thought of them doing this was disgusting.

"I told you, didn't I?" Grandma said, as I was brushing her hair because she said her scalp was itching. She had dandruff and I offered to wash it for her but she said she could wait another week. Turned out, my older sister, Valerie, who was sixteen, did not listen to our mama because she went and got herself pregnant and Mama told her she was not raising it in her house, which was why she made Valerie move in with her boyfriend, Mookie, and his family even though they lived right across the street.

That day Grandma had some kind of pie in the oven. Grandma always had something in her oven, even on hot, humid days. She would just set the oscillating fan on a chair in the kitchen doorway so the heat wouldn't blow into the living room. But I don't think it ever got that far because the kitchen sunk down low, as if it had been connected to the house later instead of all at once and the air didn't know this. The linoleum was still torn in places even though Uncle Coots had nailed it down so it wouldn't lift. In the living room, the wooden planks showed through it like maps of different countries. I always wondered why they just didn't get a big rug. How much could it cost?

"Grandma bought you something," she said, like she'd been keeping a secret but just couldn't keep it a minute longer.

"What is it?" I asked, all excited.

"Open that drawer over there," she said, pointing to her junk drawer.

As I was about to reach, she said, "No, not that one! You

know that's my junk drawer, chile. Ain't nothing in there I would want to give you."

So I pulled the other one out, which took my pushing it in hard and then yanking it out fast because the drawers were always stuck. I saw a little gold box that looked like she'd had it a long time because the gold looked more like bronze. I took it out.

"What is it?" I asked, scared to open it.

"If I wanted you to know I woulda told you. Open the box, chile."

And I did.

It was a small gray braid.

I wasn't sure what to say.

"That's your grandma's hair."

"What do you want me to do with it, Grandma?"

"Keep it. For when you get old. I want you to put a piece of yours next to it and give it to one of your kids."

"But why? And what if I don't have kids, Grandma?"

She pushed my hand away and turned her head to look up at me. Her eyes were glassy, the whites were too brown, and she said, "You will unless you can't. I don't mean to sound like I'm playing favorites but your brother and that sister of yours don't act like they have no interest in carrying on what they call our legacy even though we don't have one yet. You seem to have good sense. And you nosey. This should remind you to stay on the right path."

"Okay, Grandma," I said, although I had no idea what she was talking about. What path? I just remember saying thank you and kept greasing her scalp.

School was out. I was in Girl Scout camp and finally learning how to swim, so I hadn't been going to Grandma's as often. She had lost some more weight and Uncle Coots had told me she was taking medication for it.

"What kind of medication?" I asked.

"It's just something in her chest. She's been wheezing. But she'll be okay."

I had often heard a rumbling in her chest when she laughed and it sounded like some words were climbing up the back of her throat and were then trying to run off her tongue. But I knew a lot of people who made this same sound. They called it asthma. And even though I had finally started to like Uncle Coots, there was something about him that I just didn't trust. Of course I would learn that people sometimes lie to protect you, but it never works out that way.

The swim instructor had a death in the family and had to drive all the way to Detroit for the funeral so our swimming lessons were canceled, which is why I decided to take the bus to Grandma's, at least as close as it got. I couldn't call her because our phone had been cut off and I thought she would like it if I surprised her, which was why I decided to come through the alley instead of up Van Ness Street.

I opened the screen door and moved the fan out of the way. I called out to Grandma but didn't get an answer. The kitchen was clean, and I could see that she had not had her tea or port today. There were no cups or bowls or saucers in the sink, which meant she had not had her oatmeal. The faucet was still dripping, which meant that Uncle Coots had not found the wrench he said he needed to tighten the round thing that would make it stop.

When I walked in the living room, the television was on and the front outside door was open so I could see through the screen door and when I walked out and pushed it open, she wasn't out there. I knew something was wrong, but I didn't know what to think. I picked up Grandma's phone, which was on the couch and not on the floor where it usually was, and called my mama but I forgot she was cleaning the rich white folks' house on Lake Shore Drive today and I didn't know their phone number.

I sat down on the couch, crossed my legs and arms, and the back of my knees felt the sweat running down into my socks. I already knew Grandma was dead. Because I felt it. Nothing in this raggedy house moved. I couldn't hear the clock ticking. No cars were passing by. And for a split second I looked to see if maybe Miss Elizabeth might be home. I started walking home. Which would take about forty minutes but I didn't care because I was not in a hurry. I saw people I knew and someone offered me a ride. At a stop sign, I saw Uncle Coots sitting on a bench outside the pool hall, his hat was cocked to the side but also hiding his nose. I got out and tapped his thigh and he almost budged but I could smell the liquor, which was stopping him from moving any faster.

"Is Grandma dead, Uncle Coots?"

He looked at me and nodded. His eyes were wet and red. I took off his hat and saw rows of skin on his forehead moving up and down and then they froze.

"That damn asthma is what took her," he said. "The ambalance didn't get there fast enough."

I sat down on the bench next to him. He squeezed my hands so hard it hurt.

Death was not fair, is what I remember thinking when I looked at the ugly burgundy casket with the white satin puffed up all around her and her hands folded in a crisscross like she was trying to decide what she was going to do next. The rows of silver clasps looked like they were ready to pop.

I stepped outside where a crowd was sitting down on fold-up

chairs and I thought I heard Miss Elizabeth say, "She could've picked a better dress and who did her hair?"

"Oh shut up, Miss Elizabeth!" I yelled, which caused my mama to come over and give me a hug.

"Mama's in a better place now, baby."

"That is not true and you know it. Fuck heaven!" I said, and pushed her away, which made everybody turn to look at me but no one did anything or said anything, not even my sisters and brother or my daddy and mama. But then I saw a herd of people coming toward me with their arms stretched out and I stood up and ran into the house and locked the front door and walked over to where Grandma was still sleeping, her gloved hands folded on top of each other, and I kissed her on the cheek and sat down on the couch and just waited for her to tell me what to do next.

Working as a freelance word processor gave McMillan the flexibility she needed as she worked toward her dream of publishing a short-story collection and eventually a novel. Her mantra was "visualization is the beginning." "Every 28 Days" was written during her 1983 fellowship at the MacDowell writers' community in Peterborough, New Hampshire. Even while in residence there, McMillan had to travel home for a few days to earn money to cover her bills. The story is raw and as controversial now as it was then. Her courage to write the world she saw reveals McMillan perfecting the tools she'd been learning in fiction seminars.

Every 28 Days

"Did you get it?"

"Nope, and it's not coming, I just know it."

I

The first time it didn't come I stuck my fingers inside the hole between my legs, trying to make more room for the blood to slide out. Knew I should've made him stop at the drugstore on the way out to his beach house. But no. We were in a hurry, and when I walked into the bedroom, I could already hear the waves slapping and sloshing against each other, and my body temperature rose as I fell across the fur bedspread, and then inside the fur on his chest.

"We *really* shouldn't. We should've stopped at the drugstore first. This isn't safe."

"I'll pull out, don't worry, baby, I know when to pull out."

This was only the third time I'd been in any man's bed, and being more concerned with how well I performed than anything else, I opened up as if I'd been sitting in a dentist chair waiting to get a cavity filled.

Ten days later I sat in my living room on the couch and looked at the calendar. It was the twenty-third. It was supposed to be here yesterday. I couldn't stop looking at my stomach. It was still flat. But I imagined a baby floating around inside me. Just what the hell I needed, a damn baby.

The next day my panties were still clean. Not a drop of pink or brown or red in the crotch. We had passed right by the store, and it would only have meant flicking on the right turn signal and pushing on the brakes. Too much trouble. I was mad, and stood in front of the mirror and slapped my face. Hard. Then I started crying for being so stupid.

"You stupid bitch!" I screamed at my image. "Stupid stupid bitch!" Without thinking, I ran to the telephone and called Donald.

"It didn't come."

"It'll come, don't worry, baby, just don't worry," he said. "And if it doesn't, Reetha, don't worry, I'll be one proud father."

"Father? No, you won't either. I'm not ready to be a mother yet, Donald. I'm only eighteen years old. I'm too young to be anybody's mama. I just left Mama's house nine months ago, so please, cut this father stuff out, would you? I'm not having it, Donald."

"Honey, are you sure that's what you really want to do? I can take care of you both. I love you."

"But, Donald, this is a mistake. I don't want your baby, don't want anybody's baby right now. I'm registered for sixteen credits and I can't go wobbling into class with a stomach hanging off me that won't even fit under a desk. I'll never get through college with a baby, and besides, I can only concentrate on one thing at a time."

"Okay, okay, if that's what you want, how much will it cost?"

"Three hundred fifty dollars. Even if you can only pay half, that would help a lot."

"I'll bring it over tomorrow."

"No, please, can you bring it over today?" When he said yes, I hung up.

The welfare office was full. Women with stomachs like giant jelly beans stood around and sat hurled over in hard brown chairs. They looked miserable. I told the woman at the counter that I was pregnant and didn't want to be. She looked relieved, and made me fill out what seemed like hundreds of forms. I took a number and sat down. I felt ready to throw up again, so I filled them out hurriedly.

"Come back in three days and pick up your stickers," she said. And in three days I was the first woman in line when they opened the front doors.

"This should cover the entire procedure, honey, and don't you worry one bit. It'll be over before you know it." When I saw my name punched out in little dots, I realized that I was scared. I had never gotten rid of anything before, except a bad cold.

The next day I woke up at seven and caught the bus to the psychiatrist. At ninety dollars an hour I explained—in thirty minutes flat—why having a baby at this time would damage me psychologically. He made me write down everything I'd just told him to make sure I wasn't lying about the mental disorders in my family, and all the other diseases I could think of that no one in my family had ever had. I convinced him that if I had a baby now it would destroy my entire future. I knew if he thought I was just another irresponsible teenager, he could make me grow up in nine months. He xeroxed the letter and gave me his recommendation to take to my gynecologist. A week later I was wearing a thick white sanitary pad.

Donald had been phoning me daily to find out when and where I was getting it done, but I kept telling him soon and I didn't know where yet. Finally, I got tired of stalling, and told him that I'd had it done, that I could never sleep with him again without being reminded of this, and that he could save the flowers he'd bought me. He couldn't understand why I felt like this, and I couldn't explain it. I changed my number to unlisted and have never heard from him since.

II

"Girl, I *really* blew it this time," said a girlfriend.

"What, don't tell me you're pregnant?" I asked.

"How'd you know?"

"What else could it be? You keeping it?"

"Keeping it? I don't even know whose it is."

"Well, all I can say is that I don't ever want to go through it again, ever, even though I didn't feel a thing. I'd like to have a kid one day, I just wish I didn't have to pray every twenty-eight days that my period will come until I do."

"But does it hurt, Aretha?"

"I'm telling you, you don't even feel the needle, you're fast asleep. Just make sure they give you that laughing gas. It doesn't really make you laugh or anything, but it knocks you out. I don't think I could bear watching them do it; I've seen too many episodes of *Ben Casey*."

"I'm scared, Reetha."

"I was too, but you have to block it out of your mind. *You* made the mistake. *You* didn't take the responsibility of looking out for your own body, and now *you've* got to pay. Just think of how scared you'd be if you had to figure out how to feed it by yourself. You like welfare?"

"No, I don't want to go on welfare, I can do better than that."

"Well, what were you using?"

"My diaphragm."

"Are you sure you put it in, or are you bullshitting me?"

"I don't have to lie to you. I put the damn thing in. I always put it in."

"Well, do this, and you better do it fast. Find something much more reliable."

III

"Do you have to use that sloshy stuff tonight, baby?" asked Art. "It tastes horrible, and the shit burns. What'd you say the name of these pellets were, Oncore?"

"Encare. And they aren't supposed to be as effervescent as the other ones we've tried."

"Effervescent my foot, my lips are burning up and my penis feels like it's about to fall off. Look at it, it's red. Do me a favor, baby, please don't buy any more of this fizzy stuff. We gotta find something that does exactly what it's supposed to do and doesn't give us all this extra shit."

"I'm sorry," I said, as I pushed away from him to my side of the bed.

"It's not your fault. You sure you don't want to try a different kind of pill? They've got a lot of new ones."

"You want me to dry up again or catch cancer?"

If I could've taken the pill, it would've made life so much simpler. But they brought out the true bitch in me. Tried at least six different kinds too. The first time I lasted three whole months and just got fat and blew up something terrible. The second time lasted almost six months and I wouldn't let Art put his hands on me. Marijuana didn't work; tequila didn't work, not even co-caine.

"Get off those pills," he said. "You weren't like this before you started taking them, we have to try something else."

"Well, what do you want me to do now? So, I can't take the pill. And you say you can feel the diaphragm, so that's out. You say the foam is too messy, and rhythm, forget it."

But it was the last time that really did it. I got white splotches all over my face and looked dead. My breasts ballooned—which I didn't mind but I still didn't want him to put his fingers within one inch of my nipples. I gained fifteen pounds and felt like a pig.

And when he did slide inside of me, I was completely numb. When I read the reactions to these latest pills, and it said that it could decrease my libido, I didn't know what they were talking about. When I found out, I had to explain it to Art in plain En-glish.

"It means I don't want to make love because it nauseates me and I can't get wet when you touch me because these pills are forcing me to stay dry. They are deadening all my sensuous mem-branes and you can see they're working quite well."

But too many dry nights can kill you, so I started using those little white eggs you insert inside you ten minutes before you do it and if it doesn't happen in ten minutes, this white foam runs down your legs, soaking right through your blue jeans or your pajamas, and even in front of your own boyfriend, this is embarrassing. And my girlfriends have told me that it's even worse if you're cavorting with a potential spouse and he finds out how prepared you are for the situation.

IV

"You should get a loop," my big sister advised me. "I had one before the kids, and it only hurts when they put it in. But after that, you can do it anytime and anywhere you want to and your period is guaranteed to come."

"What kind of loop?"

"The Copper 7 is real good."

"Copper? Stuck inside of me? That really doesn't sound right to me. I mean, it's enough that a big fat penis is moving all around in there four and five times a week, how's he gonna get past some copper? And doesn't copper rust and tarnish, turn green or something?"

"Aretha, don't be so stupid. It's just a teensy weensy thing and they slip it behind your cervix. He doesn't even feel it, and you can hardly even see the thing."

"If you can't see it, how do they find it when they want to get it out?"

"There's a little string attached to it that hangs."

"String and copper? Honey, I don't need all that stuff up inside of me for twenty-four hours a day. If God had meant for it, he'd have installed it himself. Shit, I might just decay, and he could get pinched or bruised. A girlfriend of mine got pregnant with one of those things in her, but hers was plastic. Guaranteed to prevent babies, and the girl had cramps so bad when she did have her period that she couldn't even hold a decent conversation. The killer is, she had to make up her mind which she wanted to keep, the baby or the loop."

"Stop lying, Aretha, you can't get pregnant with a loop."

"I'm telling you, it happens all the time. Even Art's cousin, you know, the one with the size 50s, well, she not only got pregnant with one inside her, but had to get everything taken out. Loop. Baby. Tubes. Ovaries. All of it. And, honey, that girl's been celibate ever since. She told me that fucking was just entirely too much trouble."

V

I lay in our bed and rubbed my stomach. It was hard and swollen and it hurt because I had been holding my breath, trying to keep it sucked in. I looked over at Art. Why couldn't this be in his stomach? Why does all he have to do is get hard, stick it in, come, roll over, and go to sleep?

Why is it that none of this shit I use works?

It was four o'clock in the morning and we had just made love with this baby in my stomach. I was hoping and praying that he would do it to me so hard and so long that it would fall out, and with it would come my own welcomed blood and I could save myself some grief. But I couldn't tell him that he wasn't only making love to me, but also his child. I rolled over and finally fell asleep.

"I'm getting rid of it."

"Don't get rid of it, Reetha, please. You promised if it ever happened we would keep it. You promised."

"What do you want, to see me sitting around here bitching all day with a fat out-of-shape stomach while you're out fucking nineteen-year-olds? She'll be much cheaper than me and a baby, I can tell you that much. Can you afford to feed a child? Hell no! You can't do anything but screw and sail your stupid boats. Barbecue and fish. Tell good jokes. And what's the kid gonna tell his kindergarten teacher when she asks him what does your father do, Howie? Tell her that he sells cocaine three nights a week and on weekends when he's not skiing or sailing? And you said I promised. Well, you promised to get a real job, didn't you? You promised you'd only be doing this for six months, didn't you? You broke all of your promises, and if you want a baby, have it yourself."

He jumped up from the bed and walked into the closet. Pulled out a metal hanger. "Well, shit, you don't have to put yourself through all this trouble. Why don't you just let me scrape it out of you right now. Save us a lot of money." He started untwisting the top of the hanger and his eyes popped out of his head like a maniac. I had never seen him show his hurt before.

He started banging the hanger against the wall and I started screaming and crying and couldn't stop, like the women in the Baptist church do when they get the spirit. I saw tears all over his face, and I rolled over and hid under the pillow, buried my head deep into the mattress. I heard the door slam and then his car engine gunning and gunning and he screeched away.

I held my freezing body together with both arms and rocked as if I were in a cradle. Please come back and hold me. I'm cold in here. I'm scared. Please don't hate me. Hurt me like this. Please come back. I'll have your baby. I want us. I do, will, want this baby, your baby. Love our baby.

A girlfriend met me in front of the 7-Eleven at six-thirty that morning like we'd planned it. I had already taken the ten-milligram Valium the doctor had given me yesterday to calm my nerves and

I was beginning to feel sluggish when I jumped in her blue Toyota and fell back against the seat.

"How do you feel?"

"Terrible." I started crying again, which had become a daily ritual ever since I found out that it wasn't coming.

"Was Art still sleeping? Did he hear you leaving?"

"Yes, no. He didn't, but he thinks I'm just going to the doctor because of an infection. Besides, I gave him a little something since it's obviously safe and he never hears anything after he comes. He's as good as dead."

"You scared?"

"Yes, I'm scared. I know I'm gonna get it for this. I just know it. One day when I really do want to have a child. One day when I'm in love with the right man and we're happy and I'm working and settled in my career, boo, it's gonna happen and it's gonna come out all fucked up. Probably no hands or arms or legs, or somethin, and I'll probably never be able to have another one."

"Please, Aretha, spare me the drama, would you? This is only your second time. You're doing better than me."

"I just hope it doesn't hurt. I've never been awake before, have you?"

"Nope, and don't want to be either. I've got a loop, and aside from the cramps, I love it. I've had it in almost a year now, and no slip-ups. But if I end up getting pregnant again, I don't care whose it is, I'm keeping it. No more snatching out the little bundle from my body and throwing it in the trash or using it for laboratory studies. No siree."

My head is falling off my shoulders as they wheel me into the light blue room. They stick a plastic needle in my veins, I feel the inside of my mouth expanding, and they tell me to count backward. An abortion, oh, is that all? Baby number two. Make it quick, would you? I gotta go to work in the morning. One hundred. Oh, it is morning? Well, screw it, tomorrow. Go to work. But dinner? Is my dinner burning? Oh, shit, Art wanted steak tonight, and all we'll have is baby meat. Forgot to take the steak out of the freezer. Fish. Ninety-eight. Steak, stick. Me? Go ahead, stick me, I dare you to stick me. Ninety-seven. Yeah, I'll knock that stick off your shoulder, heffa, cause I was first in line and you know it. Ninety-six. Step across that line and I'll beat your brains out. Ninety-five. Cheater.

Art was still asleep when I got home. I slid into bed under his arm and he pushed his hand over my left breast and pushed down gently on it. My hands fell to my empty stomach. He woke up and I felt him move his warm penis against my hip, and I turned toward him, kissed him, and politely said, "No."

"What's wrong, sweetie?"

"The doctor said I have vaginitis, and I have to stick suppositories up me for two whole weeks and can't have *any* sex whatsoever."

"What's vaginitis?"

"It's a fungus. It's about bacteria. All women get it sooner or later and I can give it to you if we make love. It would make you itch, maybe even bleed if it got to that stage. You don't want it. And it's not something I would want you to have. And say, for instance if a man had a girlfriend and he was sleeping with someone else on the side, he could pass it on to her. And if she's a teenager, she might not ever be able to get rid of it because they don't know what to look for, not like an experienced woman like myself would. And besides, the man has to go through this incubation period for two weeks in order for the bacteria to dry up. And if he did give it to another woman and she ever found out who it was, she could sue the bastard."

"Ohhhhhh," he said, and rolled over, went back to sleep, and crisscrossed his hands between his own legs.

VI

When John unzipped my blue jeans, I fell against the smooth wall and my mind was full of dust and hot clouds and my eyes were seeing blue swallows sway and glide all around us.

"Is it hot enough for you, baby?"

"Oh, yes, yes, please hold me," I said, as I felt him begin sliding inside me, then I violently pushed him away.

"Wait a minute! What day is it?"

"It's the fourth," he said, looking perturbed.

"Hold it, don't move," I said, running for the bathroom, when he yelled out.

"Forget it, just forget it. I'm about tired of you breaking the flow all the time to put that junk in. When are you gonna find something that's not so much of a hassle?"

"Hassle? Missing my period is a hassle? When are you gonna find something that's not so much hassle, like using your rubber, since you're always in such a hurry?"

"They're uncomfortable, and you know it, and birth control isn't a man's responsibility."

"Oh, tell me something I don't know. But at least I'm glad that you're so very fucking concerned." He started zipping his pants back up, and I realized that I didn't care, and that this was never going to end until my period stopped once and for all, or they finally invented something that would give men some of the responsibility. And when would that be? Besides, I was only twenty-six years old, and my body still craved a man's touch.

John looked so pitiful that I went to the bathroom anyway,

and when I returned, I undressed myself and let him continue crushing all my fears.

Twelve days passed and I'm watching *Saturday Night Live* and my stomach felt lumpy and cramped up. Full, like I'd just eaten a big meal. I'd had this feeling before, but I could never tell whether it meant it was coming or there was a baby inside me.

I lay sideways on the bed, my eyes steered in the direction of the TV set and Chevy Chase was telling a very funny joke, but I couldn't laugh. I was three days late. Waiting for it was all I could do. I wanted to call my mother, and ask her what had she done all these years between each of us five kids, but instead, I stuck three fingers inside me and was disappointed when they were still clear.

I drank a bottle of Chablis to anesthetize myself. I was tired of thinking. Tired of waiting. Tired of anticipating and praying. When I woke up the next morning, my bladder was full and I had to run to the bathroom. When I got up to flush the toilet, there were four pink puffy drops, like tiny clouds, floating around the water, sinking to the bottom as if they belonged there. I pulled out my super blue box of Tampax from beneath the sink and pushed it in as far as it would go. I thought I was happy, but when I lay back down on the bed, the cramps started hurting so bad, all I could do was make myself a cup of hot tea and pop two extra-strength Tylenols. I was miserable, and the thought occurred to me that wouldn't it be nice if I could bleed for a few years straight, and then get a few years off? The telephone interrupted my wishful thinking.

"So, did you get it?" my girlfriend asked. But *Sunday Morning* with Charles Kuralt was on, and he'd just announced that there were new discoveries in birth control for men's use that he would discuss in a few moments. I sat there imagining them running to the bathroom with an erection to push something inside them, or rub something on it, or swallow something, maybe even inject it. I didn't buy it. It would be too easy, far too easy.

"So did you get it or what?" she asked again, startling me.

"Oh, yeah, sure, I got it," I said. "Didn't I tell you that I used my goop?"

"Yeah, but you were still worried," she said.

"Oh, well, you know me, I worry about everything."

"Mama, Take Another Step" was originally a short story drafted for the collection McMillan imagined would be her publishing debut. After workshopping it with her cohort at the Harlem Writers Guild, McMillan was encouraged to expand it into a novel. *Mama* was released by Houghton Mifflin in January 1987.

Mama, Take Another Step

Mildred kept an axe hidden beneath the skinny mattress on a cot in the dining room next to the oil stove. She kept white lye in a brown bag under the kitchen sink; kept her butcher knives razor-sharp and since the silverware drawer had no door on it anyway, they were easy for her to get to. She finally decided a .22 wouldn't be a bad idea. Felt she should be prepared for the next crazy niggah that acted like he wanted to hurt her or her kids, all five of em.

Besides, she was tired. Her face was hurting her today and she made up her mind that this would be the last time this niggah, any niggah, would put his hands on her pretty brown face with a force heavier than a feather, than the beginning of a kiss, or mainly to just move her hair out her eyes.

Figured wasn't no sense in trying to be too cute and get herself killed thoroughly, once and for all. Specially since Crook smacked her so hard the other night outside the Shingle that she forgot her name for a minute or two. She had pushed her platinum wig back on her head making sure it was still there, looked around to make sure nobody was watching, and jumped in the back seat of the '59 pink and gold Mercury. She did not want to be within smelling distance of him so she pushed herself up into the corner of the soft pink seat and her face against the cold glass.

Take me home, Crook, she said, trying not to cry but tears were already running her makeup, streaking it like fog melting on a window. She rolled her eyes at him till the pupils stuck in the corner sockets hard, almost cracking the windows in the car, but he didn't see her else he'd have hauled off and smacked her again. I'll get his ass when I get home, she thought. Can't move in no car noway.

The whole time she was riding in the back seat all scrunched up, pushing her wig back in place (it being full of Evening in Paris cause she sprayed it everywhere to get attention, between her legs under her arms and beneath the balls of her feet). She was trying to remember exactly where the black iron skillet was positioned amongst the other pots and pans so she'd have it easy as soon as she got in the door. Didn't take but five minutes to get home, straight down Twenty-fourth Street and Crook could hardly stay in his lane. He was drunk off Orange Rock and she was on the verge but Crook had broke down her high with his hands.

Wasn't nothing unusual about this incident, though. Many a tear had escaped her eyes when she had no desire whatsoever to cry. It was a sign of weakness to her, crying was, a true and sure indication that somebody was getting next to her, the best of her, finding out her weak spots, no matter how tiny, and that only upset her even more and made her pissy mad. At that point, she would surely be figuring out how she was gonna get Crook, for making her suffer the way she did, specially when it wasn't necessary, specially when she hadn't done nothing wrong except maybe too many hellos and see-you-laters, see-you-soons.

Mildred liked to enjoy herself when she had the chance is all, something she found hard to do most of the time. Being just twenty-seven with her oldest child almost eleven, the rest falling just nine months apart, with the exception of one year, the year that one fell out of her into the toilet, made it hard. So she enjoyed herself, being friendly. Knew every Black face in Port Huron anyway, so wasn't like she was being totally flirtatious when she smiled till her lipstick cracked in the creases of her full lips, from running her mouth, laughing so hard at Willa May talking about everybody coming in the silver doors of the Red Shingle. Just being friendly. Men and women just seemed to keep taking her friendliness to the extreme, like Crook did, and she ended up paying for all of this friendliness.

Mildred, you think you're grown, don't you? Think you just too damn grown, don't you? Crook accused her.

She didn't answer.

You know you're gonna get your ass tore up. Gonna get enough of flirting with Porky and the rest of em. You my wife, you understand that? My woman, and I don't want nobody talking to you in front of my face and behind my back, down the street and shit. You understand me, Mildred? You listening to me, girl? He looked at her through the rearview mirror, his eyes hot red and bulging out the sockets. She stared right back at him, tears all dried up now, her wig now cocked to the side. She said nothing.

Crook pulled up into the cement driveway on Twenty-fifth Street, the right headlight barely missing the bark of the big oak tree on the right edge.

Kiss my ass, motherfucker. She opened the car door, jumped out, slammed it, and walked quickly up the side steps toward the porch, turned, and screamed.

I hate you I hate you I hate you!

Mildred hadn't noticed the blood on her chin, it smeared all over her blue suede coat and the white mink collar. She had cleaned a lot of white folks' houses to buy that suede coat and she knew that blood never came out, never.

All the lights were out in the house. The kids sleeping, so they thought, but as soon as they heard the car turn up the driveway, Sonia, the oldest and in charge, sprinted to the TV, flicked it off, and ordered the other four kids to hit it. Money, Vicki, Bito, and Booge. They scattered like mice to their rooms, closed their doors quickly, quietly, and dove into bed and waited. Their eyes squeezed tight, practicing sleep in case Mildred or Crook came in to check them. By that time, though, their eyes would be relaxed enough so they would appear to be in a deep all-night sleep, their eyes beneath the skin are awake, though, tuned to noise like fine pianos, waiting.

They entered the dining room from the porch. Mildred switched on the light and saw her suede coat soiled with red blood along the seams of the pockets and deep in the holes of the big blue buttons. Drops of it made the mink come to slick points in places like a wet white dog caught in the rain. Her Evening in Paris stank. She got mad all over again, ran in the kitchen, took the plastic dish rack full of dishes, threw it up in the air, and it hit the porcelain sink. Everything breakable broke, smashed in the lap of the sink; dishes hit the floor and splattered. Plates, glasses, cups, and saucers. She gritted her teeth by scraping them together, balled up her right fist, and banged it down into the mountain of broken dishes Sonia had just washed not fifteen minutes ago. Her knuckle bled but she was too mad, too annoyed to look at the new blood. She could not even feel this pain.

Oooooooo, she screeched, you just irks me so. Always making a mountain out of a fucking molehill, thinking things is happening and ain't nothing happening. You can't see for looking sometimes. Lord, I keep saying, Mildred, leave this pitiful excuse for a man. I keep saying, Mildred, he's no good, rotten, sorry. But no, can't leave him with five babies to feed. Lord have mercy, if somebody could just show me the way.

She looked at him, shaking her head, her eyes moving like loose marbles, like magnets repelling up in her head.

If I was trying to hit on somebody you think I'd be stupid enough to do it in front of your frigging face? Huh? She put her hands on her hips bravely, started taking soldier steps toward him.

But you know what, yeah, I'd love to screw Porky, Gus, Joe Porter, Swift, and who else am I suppose to be flirting with, yeah, I'd love to fuck em all!

Mildred, shut up, you better shut your mouth, girl. You know you gonna get it, don't you? he said with his finger pointing at her like an arrow. But Mildred didn't care cause whether she kept her mouth shut or opened she always got it anyway. Either a fist pushing against her face, the back of his hand upside her head, his black steel-toed boots up her ass, something, anything that hurt.

Where's my belt? Crook said out loud, really talking to himself. He walked to the bedroom, acting almost sober now, found his thick brown leather belt, and came out the room. Snapped off the light in the dining room and gestured to her. She was trying to move backward but was already in a corner. Her heart thumped like thunder, like it was trying to issue up some courage, some guts, but it didn't work.

Since you so damn smart, let's see if your ass is as tough as your mouth, girl. Now get in here. You know you deserve this ass-beating stuff, don't you?

Crook, please, I'm sorry, I didn't mean none of the stuff I just said, Crook, please, she begged. Don't hit me, please, Crook, I promise, Crook, please. But it doesn't work.

Come on in here. He snatched her by the wrists. Think you so cute, don't you?

His face changed into the devil. He walked up to her closer, snatched off her wig, made her drop her coat to the floor, her cream knit dress, her girdle, and threw her across the bed. He kicked the door closed with his foot and the kids listened to her screaming through the thin walls, crying like a baby.

Crook, no. Crook, please. Whap. Crook, no. Whap.

Didn't I tell you you was getting too grown? Whap.

Yes, she moaned.

Don't you know your place yet? Whap.

Yes yes yes. Whap.

Don't you know nothing about respect? Whap. Bitch, you gonna learn. Whap. Teach you. Whap.

Sonia hushed the kids all huddled on the bottom bunk bed.

Shut up before they hear you, Money, she whispered loudly. Stop that whimpering before they hear us and we be next.

She tried to wrap Vicki and Bito in her skinny arms, tried to relax them but it didn't work. They all sat on the cold metal of the bed where the mattress didn't touch, whimpering, sniffling quietly, listening to the muffled noise of physical pain being imposed on their mama.

They waited for a new sound, the next one, and hoped to hear nothing, a sign it was all over and they could go to sleep once and for all tonight. There was finally quiet in the house and the refrigerator is humming, flipping ice cubes into the tray, Prince yawning on the back porch, even settled on his bed of old blankets for the night.

Money went back to his room, flipped the mattress over, and

changed his pajamas, which were soaking wet from peeing in his bed. Vicki and Bito climbed up to the top bunk, Sonia and Booge slid under the sheets at opposite ends. They all lay there, not moving to scratch, to twitch, so they could hear. Minutes passed and squeaking sounds from their parents' room. Sonia and Booge opened their eyes immediately, staring at the imprints of Vicki and Bito's little butts sagging in the mattress above. The squeaking got louder and louder, faster and faster, and muffled moans got louder and louder and then stopped suddenly, abruptly. The house was dead, finally. No squeaking, no crying, no moaning. Dead.

In the morning Crook would smile at the kids like nothing ever happened. Mildred got up real early, put a diaper on her head, put on some new pancake makeup, and smeared peach lipstick over her lips to cover up the cut, but it never worked. The kids noticed it and the dark patch of skin beneath her eye, stared at their mama like she was a stranger they were trying to identify.

What y'all looking at? she snapped. Y'all some nosey kids. Look at this house. It's a mess. Brush your teeth, wash your dingy faces, Sonia, cook some oatmeal for these kids and I want this house cleaned up before it gets dark. Don't ask me no questions about those damn dishes, just pick em up and throw that shit away. When y'all finish this house go on outside somewhere and play. My nerves ain't this long today, she said, snapping her fingers. And, Sonia, before you do anything fix me a cup of coffee first.

Crook always had somewhere to go the next morning that he made seem so important but he always just came home late evenings, drunk. First he would ask, slurring his words, where his dinner was, slobber dripping out the corner of his mouth, leaning up against anything that he was standing next to that would hold him up. Most times his dinner was there and most times he'd fall asleep on the bed with his clothes on before one of the kids could bring him his plate. Mildred got tired of not only cooking for him but doing anything whatsoever to please him. She said fuck it.

Eleven years of this kind of happiness lurked throughout her mind and body, so much that she avoided the mirror altogether unless she had on her pancake makeup, her partial plate, a rag on her head, and some Visine in her eyes.

If she had two or three dollars Mildred would send the kids to the movies. Maybe even tell em to stay and watch it twice. They didn't care what was playing and neither did she. Just get out the house. If she didn't have enough money she would tell them to look on the back porch under the steps and find some pop bottles, take em to Joe Fidell's. There they'd get two cents apiece for them and if it didn't add up so all five of them could go, Mildred would borrow fifty cents from Herman and Beulah Bell next door. They always had money. They had good jobs.

Just get out this house, go do something, leave me alone today would you? she demanded. Crook was already gone, left early to play bid whist or something with his brother Stinky and his wife, Geraldine. Mildred couldn't stand to be around either one of them, cause Stinky drank until he got fresh with her and she had to cuss him out or he was always ready to beat up Geraldine, and she drank more than he did, missing her can when she spat out her snuff most times. They enjoyed fighting. Were both trifling to Mildred, loud, uncouth, like untrained animals. She only played cards with them when she couldn't find a good partner who wanted to play all night.

Good, Mildred thought as she finally collapsed on the green satin couch, some peace and quiet. No kids. No Crook.

She looked around the house, scanning its beige walls, its

hard brown floors and clean-paned windows. This is my house, she thought. I worked too damn hard for this no-count man to be beating on me all these years. Ain't paying no bills and acting like he own me and this place. Putting his hands all on me, hurting me, when I pay the bills, the house note. I pay the little boys to cut the grass, trim the hedges. I'm the one who scrubbed white folks' houses in St. Clair, on Strawberry Lane, and way out in Marysville on my knees till they turned raw and burned, to get the weeping willow trees laid, to lime the garden, pave the driveway, and plant the flowers that's growing in the shade right now in the front yard. I'm the one who cooked Elias Brothers Big Boys and slung coconut cream pies across the counter to folks I couldn't even stand to look straight in the eye cause they was sitting at the counter and I was standing behind it smothered in grease and smoke. I'm the one who got corns and bunions on my feet from asking them sorry niggahs at the Shingle if they want another rum and Coke, the fried chicken was good tonight, Perry cooked it, and dripping barbecue sauce all over my good pumps trying to carry three plates of ribs without dropping them on the pool players. All you did was hang off the back of a city garbage truck when you felt like it with one hand at that, half drunk, waving at people. Can't even remember how many days I even seen you sober. Not more than a day I know, and you never even tried to pretend neither. Never even made up no excuses about what you did with your money, not even enough to help when the lights got cut off, here's two dollars for some pork and beans for the kids, you'd say, and if it's some change left, buy em some vanilla wafers. Never even worked long enough to earn no damn vacation pay. And what about a vacation? Who in the hell has ever had one in this house? And you got the nerve to be bragging about how pretty and healthy and smart your kids are. Don't they have your smile, your color, your high cheekbones. Ain't your fucking kids, these is my kids. I'm the one who taught em how to clean their ears, how to stop peeing in the bed, wiped their snotty noses, boiled water to give them all baths, combed and braided their hair, softened their bodies with Vaseline. I'm the one who bought the dolls the strollers the ice skates, the one who turned secret tricks with them mens from Canada to sneak in red bikes and wooden sleds and plastic skis at Christmas. The one who held you when you stumbled and almost knocked the whole damn tree through the sunporch windows, star and all. The kids could've woke up, you could've broken up their dreams of Santa Claus. Stupid. But you didn't even remember it was Christmas, didn't even remember if we'd gone shopping in the first damn place, said we could do it tomorrow. Shit, make Christmas another day you said. No, you ain't coming back here no more. Don't make no sense. My head hurts, my heart hurts, and me and my kids can do a whole lot better than this without your ass, just like we was making it before you went to the sanitarium. I was feeling sorry for your poor TB ass then. I was stupid for letting you come back in here, so stupid I could kick myself in the ass.

She gritted her teeth, shook her head in disgust at what was now pure, total, and full anguish. And it was putrid, had turned army green and she hated green unless it grew from the ground up.

Mildred came in the side door and kicked off her white leather hospital shoes. The kids sat on the sunporch watching television.

Hi, Mama, they all said in succession. She didn't return their greeting.

Sonia, unzip this dress, would you? When I change my clothes I want y'all to turn that TV off, I gotta tell you something important and I want you to keep your mouths closed and listen. Whether you want to or not.

Sonia unzipped the white nylon nurse's dress. Mildred threw the little white cap on the dining room table, revealing the red bleached hair pressed flat against her scalp.

Mama, what's that yellow stain on the front of your uniform? asked Sonia.

Girl, why you always asking so many questions soon as I come in the door? I'm tired. Them old white folks got on my nerves today and I'm tired. That old bitch, Mrs. McIntosh, threw up on me today and all over the damn bedroom floor, on the sheets, and I had to pick up her old wrinkled ass to change the sheets, change her nightgown, her bedpan, and put her back in that bed. I'm sick of that place and I'm so tired of smelling old people I could just scream. Get me a beer, would you?

She slipped out of her dress, baring her strong back and full breasts, wearing her ninety-nine-cent bra that did not support her fully, white stitches circling her breasts to the tips making white points. She is the only female in the house with breasts and she doesn't try to hide them from her daughters and her only son.

Her friends, Curly May, Gingy, Beulah, and Faye Love, would sometimes gossip about her too.

Mildred cusses too much in front of those kids, don't you think so, Shug? Faye Love would ask.

She needs to watch her mouth in front of those kids, they repeat things and one day they're gonna repeat the wrong thing and she's gonna hurt one of em, poor things.

Yeah, and since she put Crook out she be having different menfolk over there. I know, cause I be watching those different cars in her driveway too when I go outside in the morning to pick up my paper. Did you know Spookey Petty was over there the other night? Yeah, girl. Those kids gonna be all messed up in the mind if she don't hurry up and either take Crook back or figure out which one of these mens is gonna do the most for her and those kids. It ain't right, it just ain't right, Shug said, shaking her head and sipping on her cold coffee.

But Mildred didn't bite her tongue and would tell Shug, who was her sister-in-law, to raise her kids the way she wanted to and let her do the same. Shut her right up.

These is my kids, Mildred would say, this ain't half the shit they gonna see in this world and ain't half the shit they've seen already, so might as well let them find out now what's going on before some ignorant ass out in the streets gives it to em wrong and then they'll end up really catching hell. I don't want my kids growing up stupid and ignorant like some of these ill-bred little heathens running out in the streets. I don't have no stupid kids noway, they know what to think, I'll give em that much credit.

Mildred sipped her beer from the brown Stroh's and sat deep on the green couch, the kids still on the sunporch floor, turned facing her, the TV off and the screen green now.

Now, y'all kids know that we've been through a few hungry days and ain't none of y'all starved yet, have you?

The kids all shook their heads in unison. No, Mama, we ain't starved.

Well, sometimes you have to do things you don't want to do to make things right when they're wrong, you know what I mean?

They all shook their heads up and down to signify their understanding but they didn't know what she really meant for the most part.

Ain't y'all tired of this town? she interjected. Wouldn't y'all like to make some new friends and go to a nicer school? She did not give them time to answer. The reason I'm asking this, telling you this, is because I talked to your uncle Rudy out in Arizona, Phoenix, and he wants us to move out there. Said they got better jobs more money and cheaper houses and it don't snow out there. Y'all can swim all year round.

But, Mama, Sonia shrugged, I just tried out for cheerleading this year, it might be my only chance.

I don't want to go to no Arizona, Money squealed, what will we do with Prince? What about my bike? What about Chucky and Bernie and BooBoo, Big Boy and Little Boy? Ain't gonna have no friends in Arizona. It's hard to make friends.

Vicki, Bito, and Booge go along with their older sister and brother. We don't want to move to no Arizona, they ditto. What's wrong with this house, we like this house. We don't wanna go nowhere.

Mildred balled up her fist and gritted her teeth, trying to be rational, not raising her voice.

Look, I know what you're saying but your mama needs a change, y'all do too. Sonia, you can cheerlead in Arizona. Money, you can always make new friends, boy, them little hoodlums you hang around with ain't worth nothing noway, meet some civilized folks in Arizona. I'm just trying to think this thing out and I think this is gonna be the best damn move I've made in over eleven years and regardless of who don't like it, I'm the mama in this house, and we're going, as soon as I can get myself situated.

That was that.

Three days later, Money ran away from home and Sonia had made the seventh-grade cheerleading squad at Chippewa Junior High School. The only Black girl, but Mildred was not that impressed.

Chucky, Bernie, and BooBoo found Money down in a pond of water up to his knees, crying, cold, snot running down his nose, and he said he didn't want to go home cause he wasn't going to no Arizona. He hated Arizona and he hated his mama even more.

They dragged him home before he froze to death, even tied a rope around his waist so he wouldn't run. He was scared of the beating he was gonna get when he did get home but Mildred didn't beat him, she was too hurt to beat him and seeing her only son freezing cold and wet made her hate herself for a minute, feeling it was all her fault. But she couldn't let him know this, she was too strong to let him see her hurting like this. So, she did not scold him nor did she hug him to comfort him, offer him any refuge.

Go change your wet clothes, boy, and, Sonia, make your brother some tea or hot cocoa. Would you like some hot Nestlé's Quik? she asked him, her eyes full with love but her arm paralyzed at the thought of hugging him close, scared of not letting him go. He looked just like Crook too, she thought. Had his cat eyes, his grin, and his pearl-white teeth. Hope he don't end up with his sorry ways, she thought.

Tears are in his eyes as he drinks his chocolate, but he tries to wipe them before his sisters see him cry, acting like a baby. Instead, they ask him, where'd he go? How did they find him?

He'd been gone a grand total of twelve hours before anybody even missed him. When Mildred walked him through the side door and after five minutes asked where he was, Sonia said she didn't know. She and the rest of the girls had gone looking for him, asking the Pattersons, the Millers, the Howells if they'd seen Money, but nobody had seen him all day.

Mildred called next door to Shug's and the boys went to find him. They knew where he was, behind White Rose gas station at the pond where they caught polliwogs and used them to either scare girls or just watch them grow into frogs. Used to hide back there and try to do it to girls that would come, those they could convince. Sure enough, that's where he was, knee-high in the water, maybe he had thoughts of drowning himself but the water was too cold and besides he couldn't move and it was too dark to kill himself.

Before the night was over all the kids listened to his Huckleberry Finn adventure. He proudly displayed his brown paper bag full of his few clothes and he even made up stories of where he really had planned to go. Said he was gonna build himself a hut close to the school and live there until Mildred changed her mind about Arizona. The girls thought him so brave and then got mad because you could've told somebody, they shrugged, you could've asked us to come with you. We don't want to go to no Arizona, you know that, dummy.

They all decided on the spot that they would boycott the whole idea. Just refuse to go. She would have to go by herself. Sonia and Money persuaded the younger kids that they should stick together. We ain't the one with the divorce problem, we ain't gotta get away from nobody, we like our friends. So it was the consensus that Booge would stay with their aunt Jean cause Marsha was her age. Sonia wanted to stay with the Diggins family cause they were clean and always kept food in the refrigerator, homogenized milk and plenty of bananas. The littlest ones, Vicki and Bito, would stay with Elizabeth Cates and Miss Levy cause their granddaughter Kim left all her dolls and toys in their spare room. Money would stay with their aunt Shug, who lived next door, and told Sonia he could keep an eye out on the weeping willow trees Mildred had planted for her sweet sixteen birthday party. But none of this stuff worked.

Mildred made them run to Joe's grocery to lug home huge toilet paper boxes so they could start packing.

I'm putting all this stuff in storage until we can afford to move. It's gonna cost a lot of money for all you brats and me to get all the way to Arizona, and I can't be paying this house note, feeding y'all every day, and trying to save money at the same time. Sibelle said we could stay over her house for a month or two until I get on my feet. Then we leaving.

Sibelle was her sister and had six kids of her own in a big raggedy old house. She had a husband that took care of all of them, though. He was simple and his name was Mike. Sibelle was silly too and they got along just fine. The whole family were slobs and after the kids heard this news they all frowned and got a foul taste in their mouths.

They got roaches, said Sonia.

And Gary Michael caught two mice last week in the bathroom and the upstairs bedroom, said Money.

Can't we stay somewhere else, Mama? asked Booge.

Mildred told them if they opened their mouths and said another word about the subject she was gonna beat all of their asses till they couldn't sit down.

That was that.

Originally drafted in the early 1980s and mentioned in letters written by McMillan during her time at the MacDowell artists' community in 1983, "Gossip" explores themes that will be revisited throughout her novels: trust, friendship, and the consequences of vulnerability and feelings unavoidable in real life. Extensive research efforts to determine if it was ever published resulted in dead ends.

Gossip

It was the Fourth of July and the Alliance was having its picnic at Bluewater State Park. The Alliance, I guess you could say, is sort of like the PTA without the kids. We plan things to keep ourselves busy, then do them. Since there was nothing else to do, just about every Black face in town was there. Everybody except my ex-husband, Malcolm. It figures. But everybody else was having a worthwhile time, barbecuing, drinking, eating potato salad, baked beans, collard greens, and peach cobbler. It was way over ninety degrees and so humid you had to jump in the water every twenty minutes to keep from sticking. The beach was full of at least fifty different shades of brown bodies lying all over the beige sand and half of them were stretched out under the sun and the rest under umbrellas.

I was sitting on a hot black blanket under a shade tree, trying to cool off, when I saw this tall, muscular, handsome fellow who struck my eyes more than the rib I was chewing on. So I walked over to him, all bold—cause that was one of my traits when I was drinking, and I was back to drinking at that time—and I said, "You scared of the water or you just don't want to get that beautiful body of yours wet?" He laughed, and introduced himself as Charles Lincoln. I liked him right off the bat, but that body of his was doing all the talking. Turned out, he was Mattie Kellogg's "little" brother from the City. Well, just as we were in the middle of an interesting conversation about how good the barbecue sauce was, I noticed out the corner of my eye that Myra, a six-foot-two-inch Alliance member, was staring at us like she was in some kind of trance. I gestured to her to come on over, and introduced them. Now, Myra, who's usually on the shy side, had been drinking punch that I had laced with rum, scotch, and gin. She must have been feeling pretty loose because she got closer than normal to a man and asked him without the slightest hesitation if he'd like to take a dip. Now, even though she doesn't like contact sports, she's always been an excellent swimmer and since Charles was sweating something terrible, he said yes. I would've asked him myself but I can't swim. Ain't never been particularly fond of doing things that are supposed to be fun that can kill you.

I could see them way out there in the deep water. Myra, splashing like a giant baby, and Charles, swimming against the current. He was the tallest man to hit this town since my uncle Sweets, and Myra always tried to give a man a chance to prove his worth if she could stare him dead in the face without bending down.

When they came back to shore, he dried off, thanked her for the dip, and walked back over to me where we continued our conversation. This burnt Myra up and it never occurred to me till later on, when the mosquitoes were biting and a bunch of us were sitting around a fire roasting marshmallows, just how pissed off she was. Me and Charles were huddled under my blanket because it had gotten cool. All I could see was Myra whispering back and forth in Pinky's, our ugliest member, and Lavinia's, our most whorish member, ears, like some high schooler. Sissy, our most statuesque member, had already gone home. Myra ignored me and Charles altogether.

Around here, just about every eligible and ineligible man has been passed around so many times that it gets so you don't want to be bothered even if you're dying of loneliness. Lavinia, who's Myra's half sister, didn't find this out about Malcolm till after the baby—her baby, not mine—and if she hadn't been such a sneaky Alliance member, I'd probably have let her know that in the beginning it was exciting for me, too, but after the end of our second year of marriage, he started going downhill, and there wasn't a nightgown in the house or that I didn't own that could work him up and bring him to attention.

Charles spent the night and boy, oh boy, was it worth it. I started driving to the City almost every weekend, since he worked at one of those mental institutions for teenagers and didn't get off until after midnight. It was just as well, because it gave me a good excuse to get out of this hick town.

Myra stopped calling me so regular and every time I called her to tell her something yummy about me and Charles in the love department, she'd cut me off or skip the subject completely.

I forgot to mention that Myra calls herself a writer, though she's never had anything published in a book or magazine, just those snappy little sayings she calls poems, which she glues inside cards made from construction paper, and sells for thirty-five cents at all our affairs. To earn a real living, she works in the housewares department at Sears. I used to draw the sketches for the front of her cards as a favor, since I was the only one in the Alliance with the artistic talent. Her theme was called "Womanly Ways," like it was something she was real familiar with. I have to say she was pretty good at it, I guess.

Me and Pinky, who is one of our cheapest members, had been discussing the aerobics posters at one of our meetings when Myra butted in and handed me an advertisement for a drawing contest.

"Maybe this'll be of some interest to you, Crystal," she said in a snotty tone, and that was it. I thanked her as politely as I could and kept on talking. She started talking to Sissy about something they both thought was awful funny.

Well, I entered a drawing of two voluptuous women mud wrestling in wet T-shirts, all greased up with Vaseline, and when the letter came that I'd won, I was truly shocked. The prize was $300, some free art lessons in the City, and a trip to a ski resort for two.

Since Charles couldn't get off work, I felt it only fair to invite Myra. She never did anything on the weekends anyway except sew, watch her black-and-white TV, roll up her hair, and read either the *Reader's Digest, Soap Opera Digest,* or *True Confessions* because she always told me that this kind of literature gave her ideas for "Womanly Ways."

I figured we could get back on better terms by inviting her—after all, we used to be real friendly when we were planning our "escape" from home to college, even though it was only ten blocks from both of our houses. The first day up on the slope, though, she broke her leg, and she spent the second night in the hotel room. She was reading *True Confessions* and I was drinking Jose Cuervo Gold tequila. When she seemed bored listening to me go on and on about how succulent Charles was, I went downstairs to the bar. About five o'clock that morning I stumbled into our room and she was lying there with her big white leg propped up. I felt sorry for her, but she kept shaking her head at me in disgust.

"You know, you just ought to stop it, Crystal," she said, sucking her teeth, something she did that got on everybody's nerves in the Alliance.

"I'm a grown woman, and can do anything I want when I want to, so don't lecture me." I hid under the covers and went to sleep.

For the next three months, she walked around on crutches and then had to use a cane. She never complained, but every time I saw her limping, she gave me this it's-all-your-damn-fault look. I still sorta feel sorry for her.

What I did with my $300 was start my own line of cards but I left the insides of mine blank. Figured other people besides me got imaginations, and, of course, Myra got real jealous because my cards were selling like popcorn at a baseball game, and she got even madder when I didn't ask her to write any poems for me. I didn't use that cheap construction paper either. My paper shined and I used the brightest, most brilliant colors I could find. Fire-engine red. Royal blue. Hot pink. Silver. Gold. And tangerine.

"What's your theme?" she asked me, finally.

"I don't have one."

"Why not? You need a theme."

"The only time you need a theme is when you're trying to carry across a message. All I'm doing is drawing pictures of what's growing right outside my back door. Trees and flowers and fields."

She didn't say anything to that, except, "Umph."

Charles moved in because all that traveling back and forth to the City got tiresome, not to mention expensive. We were still so much in love that after a few months he decided to quit his job and find one closer to home. I told Charles that we got our share of crazy people in this town, too, just no crazy houses. Things were kind of rough on us both for a while.

Sissy called me first.

"You better watch what you tell old big-mouthed Myra, girl, she's telling all your business, and then some."

"What are you talking about?"

"Do you want to hear it or do you want to hear it?"

"What did she say?"

"Well, she asked me if I'd heard that you'd let that trifling man move in with you after he upped and quit his little menial job at that nuthouse. I told her no."

"Myra said what?"

"You heard me correctly, dear. Not only that, but she said you've been buying him new clothes like it's going out of style, from Winkler's, honey, and that every time she sees him he's wearing something new. Said he sure ain't wanting for nothing, now that he found you. She said that you took that five hundred dollars you won and blew it all on him and that both of you stayed drunk for almost two weeks and that you stopped going to those AA meetings altogether."

"She told you about the AA meetings?"

"Girl, that's old news, everybody been known that. She told us when you first started going last winter. Anyway, she said that when you finally ran out of money, you was too shame to ask her, so you started borrowing from Pinky and Charles's sister, just to make your house note. She said you was so hard up that you'd do anything to keep a man."

"Oh, really? She told you all this?"

"Every single word of it in one full swoop."

"And you believed her?"

"Don't make a difference what I believe. Your business is your business. I got enough to worry about in my own house without worrying about what you doing. I know you ain't no fool, and I know that Myra's just probably jealous cause she ain't got nobody, I bet that's all it is, cause I'm sure that deep down, she don't mean you any real harm."

"She really said all this?" I asked again, still unbelieving.

"Yeah, and don't tell her I told you, either."

Pinky called the same night.

"Sissy told me she already warned you about Myra and she told me she told you what Myra said, but she didn't tell you everything. I want you to know what kind of a friend she is."

"Wait one minute. Did you tell Myra that I borrowed money from you?"

"No, girl, I told her that you lent me some money right after you won the drawing contest."

"Why is the girl bad-mouthing me all of a sudden?"

"How the hell am I supposed to know? Maybe she's depressed cause she got laid off at Sears and had to move back home with her mama and daddy. Did she tell you?"

"No, she ain't exactly been sharing her life secrets with me."

"Well, I'll tell you one thing, that girl's got a big mouth to go along with that big body of hers, and you better watch it. She told me everything she told Sissy, and no telling what she's telling Lavinia. And you know it'll be all over St. Paul AME Church if Lavinia gets ahold of any goods on you. Remember when you guys went skiing?"

"Yeah."

"Well, honey, Myra said you got so drunk that you were kissing the bartender all over and anybody else who'd buy you a drink, and that you spent the night with somebody you picked up at the bar and literally crawled through the door of the hotel room."

"You can't be serious."

"Yes, I am, and she said you're a fool if you even think your ex, Malcolm, wants you back, cause you're getting too old for somebody to want anyway."

"You have to be lying, Pinky."

"If I'm lying, I'm flying."

Charles's sister, Mattie, finally called.

"What's this I hear, girl, about you turning my brother into a pimp and an alcoholic or something?"

"Mattie, come on, don't tell me she's been calling you, too."

"Who?"

"Myra."

"No, but I heard it from Sister Moncrief in church, who knows the mama of the girl that watches Lavinia's baby when she works. Word is out that you turning your house into a still, and almost holding my brother captive. Buying him all kinds of clothes to keep him, and that ever since you won that six hundred dollars in that contest, you been acting strange, and the biggest word out is that you been doing more than taking art lessons down in the City when you hop down there on Thursday evenings. Tell me all this mess is stupid so I can ease my mind, Crystal."

"Forget all this mess, Mattie, you should know me better than this."

When I hung up the phone I was so mad that I was shaking, and to calm myself, I pulled an unopened bottle of wine from the refrigerator that I'd been saving for company. I could've sipped as hard as any lumberjack after a hard day's work, but this time I knew that getting drunk wouldn't solve or change a thing. So I sat there, and couldn't help staring up at the map of the world tacked on the wall in front of me. I felt myself being hypnotized by the millions of green- and red-veined lines going in every direction. I found myself squinting in order to follow their path, but there seemed to be no real starting or ending point to any of them. When I felt myself moving closer, the oceans and seas were the only things clear to me.

My fingers throbbed, just itching to dial Myra's number, but I couldn't. I exhaled for a long time, and put the top back on the wine. I placed it deep inside the refrigerator. As I was about to turn out the light, a roach crawled from behind Greenland. I let it get away.

Charles finally got a job in another nuthouse, halfway between here and the City, and we got married, quietly. We moved down to the City for more privacy and I became an inactive member of the Alliance.

Myra called me every so often, like nothing had ever happened because she still didn't know that I knew how big her mouth was. And when she did call, I was distant, like a telephone operator, but Myra didn't seem to notice. Ever since we moved down here, she's been dying to come and visit. I always had some excuse why it wasn't a good time. Right after I told Charles all the things she'd said, he wasn't particularly crazy about ever seeing her again.

He went to Chicago one weekend to visit his brother and I stayed home because I had some sketching to do for class, when Myra called. I shocked myself by inviting her to come down.

She pulled up in her old four-door olive-green Skylark. I had just come in from buying some juice and a bottle of wine because the only thing in the house to drink was a fifth of gin, and I didn't think she would drink that.

She liked the apartment.

I poured her a glass of wine, and myself a glass of fruit punch. She sipped it like it was that herbal tea she usually drank at all hours of the night when she couldn't sleep. I couldn't believe how she was guzzling it, and when the bottle was empty Myra asked me if we had anything else in the house to drink. What had gotten into this cucumber I didn't know. I pulled out the gin. She started sipping that with a vengeance, and was getting ripped by the minute. Finally, she started laughing out loud, something I had never heard her do.

Then she started reciting some new poems she'd written, so I turned off the eleven o'clock news. I was trying hard to act interested, but I knew she'd taken them right out of Bartlett's book of quotations, and had just switched the words around to make them fit her new theme, which she now called "Natural Wonders."

When I noticed the glass was slipping from her hand, and her words were getting thick and running together, I asked myself, "Is this how ridiculous I looked when I was drunk?" I caught the glass before it left her grip and led her to the couch. Myra fell into the cushions, but instead of trying to take her clothes off, I covered her long body with a green blanket.

I assumed Myra had managed to get up and put on her pajamas, because from my bedroom I heard her moving around and mumbling. I guess I finally dozed off, but sprang up when I felt something crawling into bed with me, and then a set of hands sliding around my waist. I slid over to the other side of the bed like a rattler and turned on the lamp. There was Myra, her head pushing up off the pillow. She looked just like my German shepherd did when he used to wait under the table for me to slip him some scraps. I jumped out of bed and stood erect, next to the lamp.

"Are you losing your mind, Myra?"

"No, Crystal," she said, slurring. Part of me wanted to slap her face until she got sober and the other part wanted to laugh because at first I thought that maybe this was some kind of joke. My instincts told me that it wasn't.

"Come on, Myra, you can't be that drunk. What do you think you're doing in my bed?" I asked, putting my hands on my hips.

"Crystal, please, don't be mad at me. Please. I'm tired, tired of pretending. Every time I saw you with somebody new—first that mealy Malcolm, and now this crusty Charles—it made me jealous and angry."

"Jealous? Myra, come on."

"I was pretending that I liked you for my friend, but it hurt me to see you having so much fun with them and not me. We used to have so much fun together before you got so man crazy, didn't we?"

"Yeah, but, Myra, there's nothing wrong with me being man crazy, and I don't think you really want me. I've been your friend for too long. Why didn't you tell me you felt like this?"

"Because. All I want to do is be close to you, that's all. Just sleep with me tonight, Crystal, please? I promise, I won't ever tell anybody about this. I promise."

Well, first of all, I ain't never considered sleeping with a woman before and if I had, it damn sure wouldn't have been Myra. And who's to say that if I had slept with her, that it wouldn't be all over the front page of the *Times Herald* the next day that I was a married closet homosexual who had gotten turned out in her own bed by her ex–best friend whose half sister once stole her ex-husband, while her present one was out of town visiting his brother in Chicago? No, siree.

She buried her face deeper in my pillow—Charles's pillow—and started crying. I thought about all the nights she'd sat in that little dingy apartment and watched black-and-white TV, her phone never ringing with an invitation unless it was a girlfriend, reading *True Confessions,* and now, living with her folks. I realized how lonely she must feel. I wanted to hold her hand at least, but I think Myra needed much more than that.

"Myra, you can sleep in here," I said. I closed the door quietly and walked out into the living room. I really could've used a drink.

In the morning Myra took a long shower, got dressed, and complained about a hangover. She told me that she thought she had a good time, but she couldn't remember.

I could still hear her gunning the engine when the phone rang. It was Pinky.

"So, did you give her the axe, finally?"

"No."

"What? Why not? She earned it."

"Because she wasn't feeling very well when she got here. I don't even know why she drove all the way down, just for one night. I think she was coming down with a cold or something, because she fell asleep before the news came on. Didn't bother me, because I had to finish some sketches for class anyway."

"Is that all that happened?"

"Well, no, she did read me a few of her new poems, and they're really getting better."

"You mean to tell me that you didn't tell her off and kick her out of your house after all the cruel things she said about you?"

"No, Pinky, and as a matter of fact, all we got a chance to talk about was the aerobics class. Speaking of which, how many people have you guys managed to muster up?"

Written in 1985, "Curtains Up" is a "working draft" and the open-ing of a coming-of-age story. McMillan visualized it as a novel that follows the main character, Doris, from her childhood in the Midwest and on to the West Coast and the experiences she has: men she loves, loneliness, drinking, and the ones who don't stick around.

Curtains Up:
Hands-on Experience

I always liked men who were good with their hands. Even when I was fourteen, the only reason I started going with Bookie was because when the chain broke on my bike and I fell off and skinned my knees, he picked me up and took out a link so that the chain was tight. I felt saved. He had bulging muscles and a thick neck, just like a real man. He was so black he was almost purple. I found his skin color mouthwatering. He looked edible. The whites of his eyes were milky blue and he had the whitest teeth and the most gallant smile I'd ever seen on a man. He was sixteen. I stood there as the blood ran down my knocked knees, as implacable as a detour on a freeway. The root-beer-colored grease covered his hands so that his skin shone like India ink. His fingernails were yellow.

The next day, he walked me home from school the long way, through Windfall Woods. We brushed bushes away from our faces as we strayed from the path. It was so hot and moist the mosquitoes landed on our bare arms ten deep. Then he stopped as if he were waiting for a light to change. I rubbed my hands up and down my arms to busy them away. My heart pounded like somebody was banging on a door. He walked up to me, opened his fingers like two fans, and slid them around the small of my back. He kissed me. It was the softest, sweetest, juiciest kiss I had ever had in my life. It was the first kiss I'd ever had in my life and I know I turned to liquid and soaked right through the ground.

We walked this way home from the high heat of summer until the leaves turned red and yellow and then fell off the trees. Snow crunched beneath our feet and icicles hung from hard branches. Everybody could see us then, though we weren't trying to hide. No one understood what I saw in him, especially my mother. "That boy is just too dark for me," she said. "Nobody in this family ever come close to his color, and it doesn't make any sense for a child to be that dark." I disagreed with her, but I didn't argue. Bookie Washington was kind and gentle toward me. He made me feel like rolling up my hair every night. Made me daydream about his smile when I sat over my social studies book. Made me want to play Smokey Robinson's "Choosey Beggar" over and over until my mother made me turn it off.

He never raised his voice, even when he was excited. He had a voice like a lullaby and before I went to bed he whispered through the telephone that he loved me. I slept with the orange elephant he had won for me at the state fair so I could feel close to him. Sometimes I still couldn't get to sleep unless I made my-self dream about him first. I got chills thinking about tomorrow, and couldn't wait for him to put his arms around me and kiss me like we had all day.

Then my mother told me we were moving to Dayton because my father was getting transferred. "We can't move," I told her, "I've got too many friends here."

"All you're thinking about is that old nappy-headed boy," she said.

"So what, I like him a lot, and I don't want to move." She was not impressed by my emotional attachment.

"That's why God made buses and trains and automobiles, you won't be *that* far from him." She left it at that.

I ached at the thought of leaving Bookie. I loved him more than I loved her. I ached at the thought that somebody else, probably old pop-eyed Geechey or Poopie or Linda Cobb, would be next in line to get one of his luscious kisses. No telling what else. We promised to write each other, but three months after we moved, my cousin called and told me that Bookie was dead. He had been hit by an ambulance that was going through a red light as he was crossing the street. For months, I still didn't believe it. When I went back to Elyria for Christmas, I walked by his house and waited for him to come out. Another family lived there and for the first time in my life I had to teach myself to forget what I felt. This felt worse than when my cat Malcolm died.

By the time I left tenth grade, I had proved how smart I was. I maintained a high grade point average and made the varsity cheerleading squad. I had become a sports fanatic and leaned toward basketball. My best friend, Cynthia, had always thought she was beautiful, and fantasized about being a movie star, so when she joined the after-school theater club, she insisted that I join too. I did so mainly because I was bored. When there wasn't a game, I had nothing to do. We did improvisations but I found most of them to be embarrassing moments. I wasn't used to being so honest about my feelings in front of a room full of people. When I found out there was more to the stage than acting, I became more involved and interested in production so I could see the results of what I was doing as opposed to being watched all the time. I was no actress because I found it hard to pretend to be somebody else, and besides that, I had a terrible memory.

I got carried away reading plays, reading about plays, and understanding character motivation. I didn't have much of an imagination, but no one seemed to notice.

I went to church almost every Sunday out of guilt even though my mother never made me or my brother go if we didn't feel like it. Mother went to bingo on Sundays while my father watched sports. My older sister had moved to Atlanta when she was eighteen. She was married and had two kids. I felt sorry for her because she was already old. She was twenty.

The first Sunday in October of 1968 was communion at Metropolitan Baptist, like it was every month. I walked in to sit in the back row like I always did. I never missed communion because I always prayed there would be wine instead of Welch's grape juice in those little silver goblets. No such luck. Today, I couldn't sit in my usual spot because there was an entire row of brand-new, good-looking young Black men lined up on the bench. I almost tripped over one whose big feet stuck out in the aisle. When he pulled them back all five of them looked up at me and smiled. I was so embarrassed, though I didn't look in any one's face in particular because their heads were a long brown blur.

I sat down two rows in front of them. Reverend Jones announced to the congregation that we had guests today. I turned around quickly to take a peek. "These boys," he said, "are all basketball players at Dayton Community College. They are here not only to get an education and partake in sports, but because they don't want to stray too far from the Lord." The truth was their coach had forced them to come so they could set a good example for the team. I turned around to face Jesus, let the air out of my lungs, and said Praise the Lord under my breath. I spotted which one I wanted.

His name was James Johnson but everybody called him Bubbles. Boy, was he tall. He was over six feet and after church Cynthia walked up to all five of them and introduced herself. She batted her eyes like Betty Boop and imitated her mother's sexy grin. She forced me to come with her, though I tried to remain demure. One of them was incredibly ugly, and I hadn't noticed until then. Bubbles was the talker of the group, and he didn't take his eyes off me. He talked with his hands, making swaying motions in the air, and I noticed a miniature diamond ring on his pinky. He was too young to be wearing a diamond ring, wasn't he? I hardly said a word, except "Yes, I'm a junior in high school." He made me nervous. He had to be nineteen, I thought, and when he pulled his collar up to protect his ears from the stinging wind, I got a whiff of his cologne. He was wearing British Sterling, which didn't smell quite the same on my brother, Sinclair. Bubbles smelled like a man.

"This is my best friend, Doris Blackwell," Cynthia said. She was prettier than I was, but I didn't care. Besides, she had her eyes on the yellow one, Oscar, and I was beginning to notice that black must be my favorite color, because Bubbles was only a shade lighter than Bookie. We both were invited to their first game.

Not only could he dribble but he sure could shoot. I didn't know he was going to be the star of the team. I watched him run back and forth down the blond wooden floor and jump into the air like a torpedo, and whoosh. Two points. Sweat dripped down his handsome chocolate face and he never once looked into the bleachers at everybody screaming out his name. He concentrated on that ball and the men around him. I liked that. His hands grasped that orange ball as if he were giving it a silent order to follow his will. He had control. They won the first five games because he'd scored more than thirty points each time. By the third game, I had made up my mind that I wanted him to want me because I wanted him, and I'll tell you something, when I want something, I usually get it.

One of the players was having a party after they'd won the fifth game. My friend Bo-Peep was seeing him. I only went because I knew Bubbles was going to be there. I'd been invited to other college parties, but I wasn't ready to appear yet. Even after the games, I never hung around the locker room door when they ran off the floor with their towels around their necks. I did my disappearing act. I hadn't seen him face-to-face since church last fall. I heard his voice before I saw him and smelled his British Sterling, which gave me a clue as to his proximity. I turned toward the punch bowl, and dipped out a cup. I wasn't thirsty. When I noticed he was talking to another player on the team, I walked past him. "Hello, Doris, isn't it?" I almost tripped over my cuffs. I pretended like I didn't remember him.

"Yes, it's Doris. How'd you know my name?"

"I met you at church a while back." Then I pretended like it was all coming back to me.

"Oh, yes, but I don't remember your name." He went for it.

"Bubbles, but you can call me Bubs." He flashed all thirty-two at me; and I thought Bookie's teeth were white. He wouldn't take his eyes off me, and he looked dead into mine as if he were trying to hypnotize me. It was working.

"Has anyone ever told you that you've got beautiful eyes?" I blushed, even though I knew it was probably a line.

"No," I said politely, "thank you."

"I'm not kidding. As a matter of fact, you're about the prettiest young lady I've met since I've been in Dayton." He was getting beside himself now, but I was eating it all up. My chest was hurting because I felt like I was losing my breath.

Oh, my God, I said to myself. How did I look? I had made the burgundy bell-bottoms I was wearing that proudly displayed how round my hips were, and I wore a light gray nylon blouse that gave some indication that I wasn't flat chested. I tightened the burgundy scarf through the friendship ring I wore around my neck. My hair was thick and long and fell down past my shoulders and flipped up like a wave. My lips were peach.

In those days I was considered very good-looking. People used to tell my mother that she better watch out cause I was gonna be something else once I filled out. Bubbles had already noticed how filled out I was. "Would you like to dance?" he asked. It was a slow record and I knew I was going to step on his toes because I had never learned how to slow dance. I was always accused of leading when I should be following. "Sure," I said, as I sat the cup down. I did not step on his toes even though I felt intoxicated by the smell of that British Sterling drifting from his warm neck and drunk from the heat of his hands moving across my back. We danced three records in a row and when a fast one came on, I felt faint.

This was the beginning of us and no longer did I have to watch the girls wait by the locker room door praying he would escort one of them up to his room. I proudly waited for him and everybody knew that Doris was Bubbles's girl. He kissed longer and deeper than Bookie. His hands were bigger and his arms encircled my entire body when he hugged me. Only it was different with him. I couldn't stand being away from him. I thought about him all day and all night and everywhere I turned I would see his face. I played Aretha Franklin's "Ain't No Way" on my record player every night until my mother threatened to break it. I started writing poetry. Every line had a flower or a cloud or a heart in it. All my girlfriends were jealous because I was always too busy to go to Kmart or the movies with them. Even the college girls hated my guts because they wanted him too. The mystery that gathered around Dayton was what this eleventh grader was doing to keep a star basketball player so amused and delighted. To tell you the truth I didn't know.

Bubs thought I was most intelligent and constantly told me how sexy I was. He meant it, and my mother liked him because he was mannerable and in college. She thought he was going to amount to something and maybe I would get lucky. After all, I was going to graduate soon and though she knew I was going to study theater arts, she still prayed that I would find a suitable husband first and get educated later. Bubbles fit the mold.

I had written a couple of one-acts and our group had even staged a couple of them. Bubs thought I had considerable talent and was obliged to broadcast everything I did to his friends. The whole team came to see my plays. He made me feel special, like I was on a pedestal spinning around in a slow dream.

It took him a year to get me to slide out of my stretch pants on my mother's birthday. I only did it because I loved him and there was no doubt in my mind that he loved me. He told me the first night I went up to his room after a game that he would wait for me. He was so glad I was a virgin. He said he didn't know there were any left. He felt lucky. I wouldn't take off my orange nylon turtleneck because I didn't want to feel naked; besides, it was wintertime, my first time, and cold as hell in his little room.

I never knew a man's body could be so beautiful until I watched Bubbles take off his clothes. It was the first time I had seen a man naked and the symmetry of his limbs, his muscles, and his Blackness overwhelmed me. He smothered me with his long warm body and whispered, "I won't hurt you," into my left ear. I believed him until it started hurting. "Ouch," I said, but before I knew it the pain disappeared, and I became transfixed by the rhythm of his body. It sorta felt good, but I couldn't tell which felt better, him inside of me or him on top of me. "I love you," he crooned, and I sang out the same words when the roller coaster ride came to a halt. I lay there, wondering if this was all there was to it. I mean, I never saw any lightning or heard any firecrackers go off. What about those hot marshmallows that were supposed to melt between my legs? That's all Bernadine had told me about. "Girl, ain't nothing like it in the world. When you feel your body trembling and you can't do nothing about it but float away, you'll know it." All I knew was that my turtleneck was soaking and wasn't going to be dry by the time I got home.

"I want to marry you," he said. I sank into the black hole of love because I now had someone and something to look forward to besides college. We agreed that we would both get our degrees first. We lay there rubbing cheeks. His whiskers had started to grow and all I could think of was that I've got a man here in my arms. He felt so good. If I were a half circle, then he was the other half. I saw my whole life in front of me up there on his cracked ceiling.

I would have my degree in theater arts and though I knew I'd probably never be good enough to compete with those professionals on Broadway in New York City, I knew I could always teach school or work in one of those cultural programs. What difference did it make? I'd be standing right next to the other stars' wives in the bleachers after Bubs started playing in the pros. We would buy one of those big homes with a two-car garage and it would be hidden behind tall electric gates. We would travel and have money and I would have at least two kids. A boy and a girl. Bubs fell asleep and I untangled my arms from around him. I put my stretch pants back on and kissed him gently on his plum lips. If I got pregnant, which I didn't think about until I was driving home, at least I'd be out of high school by the time it was born.

But I didn't get pregnant. I won a scholarship to Whittier College in Los Angeles and Bubs was accepted into a Big Ten team at Indiana University. That June, he wrote in my yearbook: "If a lot of time goes by before we get to see each other and you meet somebody else, before you get close to the altar, call me collect before you say 'I do.'"

I met somebody in L.A., alright. A thirty-year-old, six-foot-three-inch reincarnation of Bookie. His name was David and he was a boxer and drove diesel trucks. He had a Harley-Davidson motorcycle and he wore thick black boots even in all the heat. His legs bowed and he walked like Clint Eastwood. I met him at Hermosa Beach, where I hung out every weekend. I used to lay out under the sun until my body turned the color of fresh baked bread. I would bring books out there to read, though the sun was too bright and the breeze always blew too much sand across the pages. David taught me how to bodysurf. Introduced me to a lot of white hippies and gave me my first joint. It made me sluggish and made my mind feel heavy and thick. I would sit in his window and listen to the waves and smell the ocean air until I came down. He talked me into not wearing a bra. Took me out to dinner in the spiffiest restaurants and taught me which wine to drink with what meal. He had what could've been considered a British accent, but it turned out that he was trying too hard to sound white.

With David I felt those melting marshmallows and heard thunder and saw blue and yellow lightning and a rainbow of fireworks. Every single weekend. I was addicted to his body, but as time went by he became more and more obsessed with me. He would drive all the way from the beach just to bring me flowers. He thought I was beautiful and had the best body he'd ever seen. It was my skin color that he had learned to love all over again because for the past ten years all he'd dated were white girls. He smothered me with affection and would do anything I asked him to. It got so that I would ask him to do things just to see if he would do it. He started getting on my nerves after six or seven months of pure mush, but not enough for me to leave him alone. We hardly went anywhere, not even to the beach, which was only a few yards from his apartment.

Bubbles called me about once a month and sent letters that were barely legible. His handwriting was terrible and so was his grammar. If he couldn't play basketball, Lord knows he probably never would have gotten into any college. At first I wrote him four- and five-page letters once a week, telling him about school and the plays I'd written. I had worked up to three-acts. I told him about the slinky palm trees and how hot and dry it was and I exaggerated when I told him how lonely I was. I had told David about him, but David said he wasn't going to worry about a college boy who was two thousand miles away.

When Bubs called to tell me that Indiana was playing UCLA and he couldn't wait to see me, I felt sad instead of excited. I told David that my grandmother was visiting and I wouldn't be able to see him for the entire weekend. He wanted to take us both out to dinner but I told him she was too old to sit under the air-conditioning because she had rheumatism. He believed me. That was part of the problem, he believed everything I told him.

I met Bubs after the game. I waited on the lowest tier of the bleachers for him. I was trembling. When I saw him come through the locker room door he looked like he had shrunk. The bleachers behind him went up forever and even the basket looked higher than the one at Dayton Community. My memory of us clammed up and as he approached me I forced myself to conjure up old feelings.

I felt nothing stir inside me when "You look good, Doris," was all he said. They had lost by twenty-eight points, so I figured he was embarrassed and hardly in the best of spirits.

"So do you, Bubs." We caught the bus all the way from West-wood down Wilshire Boulevard and I pointed out all the land-marks. We both felt the distance between us. The silence was pushing him toward the window and me toward the aisle. When we reached my apartment he was impressed by my swimming pool and thick carpet. He couldn't believe I had a garbage dis-posal. I hid David's undershirts and picture before I took off my jacket.

"When did you stop wearing a bra?" I looked down at my nipples pointing through my tie-dyed T-shirt and felt embar-rassed.

"Oh. I only go like this on the weekends, why? Does it bother you?" All of a sudden I wanted it to bother him.

"No, it doesn't," he said, lying. The evening dragged on and I had to drink three glasses of wine so I could get in the mood for him. I faked passion the entire night and tried to pretend he was David. I watched him sleep and couldn't believe that this was the man I was going to marry one day. It didn't feel right. He was still cute, but that didn't seem to matter anymore. It seemed like years had passed since I was in high school, sneaking up to his room and turning on the red light so we could touch in the right atmosphere. I didn't sneak anymore.

"So," he said the next morning, "have you met someone out here that you like?" I swallowed the lump in my throat and said, "No." I didn't know at that moment if I told him "yes" if he would disappear from my life altogether. I wasn't sure if I wanted him to. This blank feeling could very well pass, even though he did seem childish compared to David because all he had talked about was basketball, the Cadillac and diamond rings he was going to buy when he made the pros, and clothes. He was so hip. I couldn't picture myself with David for the rest of my life either. I didn't love him. I loved the fireworks and the marshmallows and I wasn't going to give them up just yet, not until I found a replacement and especially not now, for an old flame who happened to be passing through for the weekend.

"You don't have to lie, Doris," Bubs said, "we're both adults. You're nineteen, old enough to do what you want to do when you please. If you've met somebody, you can tell me." I figured if I told him the truth I would hurt his feelings or else that would give him the signal to tell me that he'd met somebody and I didn't want to know. So, I pulled the covers up over us and tried to re-create the past again, though the whole time I wished I were at the beach.

When David asked me to marry him I was shocked. He pulled out a diamond so big it made my eyes water. I didn't know how to tell him that I didn't like diamonds. Everybody had them and they seemed so trite. He had even picked out the church. Couldn't find the right words to tell him that I never wanted to get engaged or get married in a church or wear one of those corny white wedding gowns with a mile-long train dragging behind me on the carpet. What was the point of it all? Church weddings always felt like funerals to me. All those flowers and the organ music. Everybody crying. I always cried because the setting was so sad.

I didn't realize I felt like this until after I moved out to Los Angeles. One day I got in my little Mazda and drove all the way up Highway One toward San Francisco. I stopped in Big Sur and stuck my feet in a running brook. There were some trout squiggling like liquid silver through the clear water. I realized that all my life I had done everything my mother had told me to do. Had done everything everybody with authority told me to do, and now I didn't have to anymore. I could make my own decisions. I read books that opened me up and turned me inside out. I took a peek and my mind and imagination began to soar. I wanted to live a bold and daring life, not a safe and cozy one. I wanted to be good at something besides marriage. It seemed like such a thoughtless task. And I wanted my life to be jagged so that I could feel good when I smoothed out the edges. So I told him no.

Of course he was hurt but I couldn't help how I felt. I threw myself into plays. At night, though, I kept having this dream that one day I would fall hopelessly in love with some tall Black handsome man who would fill me up with everything I needed and we would dash off somewhere romantic and just do it. David was not him. Neither was Bubbles, and during the following summer I felt relieved when he sent me a letter telling me he was getting married. I felt sad when he also told me that he didn't make it in the pros.

I laid out under the scorching sun at Malibu. I opened the first page of Khalil Gibran's *The Prophet*. The sand blew in my face and turned the page, so I sat up. On top of a curling wave I saw an open highway ahead of me. I saw plays I would write one day and places I would go. I saw a headless man but I didn't shudder, because I knew that when I did meet him most likely he would glow in the dark.

SKETCHES
& STARTS

Never a writer who pretends to write beautiful prose, McMillan is known for telling raw and powerful stories with an unapologetic and authoritative voice. At the heart of her stories are people and places squarely centering the real world. To build authentic families and friendships, she writes about situations that people who look and love like her can share in and identify with. To tell the best stories she can, she keeps herself rooted in the reality around her. What follows are unfinished sketches of people and places, fits and starts from a writer's mind, some abandoned, some building blocks for books to come, including two characters, Myrtle of "Three Zeroes" and Buster of "Walk-By," who are central to an as yet unpublished novel.

In Spite of It

But here I am. I want to say, what you see is what you get.

What you saw is what's here. See me as a prize; do you want it or don't you?

I'm bold. I think. So bold that I scare myself sometimes. I stick my neck out because I'm afraid, and in spite of it. Look what I've lost so far. I ask myself: Should I just fall down somewhere else, squeeze all the water out of this sponge until I'm clean, freezing, shivering. No. I have already stuck my foot into a deep pool. I can swim. I can go the distance. I am afraid, but so what else is new. I have already drowned.

Rented Horses

. . . she could also hear the hoofs of horses trotting and clicking against the pavement from outside her window. She could look down over the skinny leaves of small trees that were hoping for a chance to grow before winter set in. She looked at fake riders pretending to be of a real equestrian nature and she knew it was really quite impossible to gallop in the park, where one could just as easily be hit by a car on a horse as if you were on your own two feet. She wondered why they paid a whole $15 an hour to trot when they could gallop, really gallop, in the country, let their hats fly off against the trailing wind and not care, where they could really perspire and the horse would not have to be whipped to run, it was his nature, and he too would love the openness and smell of grass and even mountains and fresh spring water. But no, they spent their Con Ed money to trot trot on crowded paths and sometimes she even wanted to get a slingshot and crouch down below the windowsill and hit them with red beans she had bought and would never cook. Just to get their attention, to get them to realize they were not as gallant as they thought on their rented horses. Sometimes she noticed them running into open car doors and weren't quite able to turn the horse around and sometimes the horses insisted on going against the red light. They are colorblind in the city. A swift stiff kick in the side ended all such desire to stop and off they went. She could see all this sometimes without looking, just by turning her ears the right way, she could tell.

Shivering

I sit in the kitchen, trying to concentrate on the paper, but my heart feels like a sponge full of hot water. Maybe I'm not dead. I just don't know.

"You shouldn't be scared," my girlfriend told me.

"I know I shouldn't," I said. "But I am. Every time I fall in love something happens to mess it all up. I just don't know."

I get up from the chair and walk to the living room. It is bare. Not a single piece of furniture. The windows are clean, and from them, I can see the tops of mountains. White. Fog like a halo over them. Over me.

Before I know it I'm shedding tears, and I have absolutely nothing to cry about. After all, I didn't ask him to tell me if he loved me. All I wanted to know was exactly how much he cared. He couldn't tell me. He said he had to think about it. As a matter of fact, he'd been thinking about it for a few days now. What was there to think about? Either he wants me or he doesn't. Either he thinks he wants me or he doesn't. Either he cares about me or he doesn't.

He's scared too. Like a prairie dog in the middle of the highway and headlights are on him too close. He can't run fast enough. But say it. Don't run from me. Don't hide from me. How many years have we both run? The wall is brick. It is hard. My heart is soft and warm. I have split it wide open for you to come on in. You put one foot in, then your head, then your arms, and I thought I saw your heart coming to join mine. Was I seeing things? Or just bleeding from old wounds? Sometimes you stick your neck out, you take a chance, you get burned. Other times, you get what you want. But who am I to tell a man what to do, how to go about loving. Perhaps I'm merely trying to perpetuate your dreams. Instead of living it in my head, on paper, in the bathroom, I want to make all of them real. I want them to exist.

Human Noise

I hate those phone calls. The fuzzy sound of long-distance hissing in your ear. First the left, then the right. The "I can't talk long, but" phone calls. Stop. I don't want to hear who just died, my ears won't listen, I'm listening, go ahead, not one of the kids, please not one of the kids. Two seconds pass. It's your grandfather. No, not him, please not him. Age should be more of a deterrent from death than anything else. He has carried me. Tickled and pinched me on my butt. Not him. The longer you live, the longer you should be able to live. It's a mark of longevity, of endurance, why take that away, at least not in pain. No pain. Send me the pain. Let it pass through his body into mine, into my veins and blood, let me pump it out for him. I'm young and strong and I know how to handle pain.

Like when I tried to jump a puddle at the curb and the tips of my red boots slipped off the edge and I fell face-first on the cement, hitting my knees and scraping my palms. It hurt, but I could get up and wipe off the pain, the dirt, the blood, and simply dirty a white napkin. I could walk it off, forget about it cause it was over.

He had a stroke? No. Yes. He's in Mercy Hospital. No. Not the death house. Ain't too many niggahs made it out of that hospital for minor ills, not a stroke. Aunt Barbara died there, so many people have died there for no reason but inadequacy. Lack of caring. Maybe no insurance or couldn't find their medical sticker for that month.

When I was thirteen, on Easter Sunday, I had a toothache that wouldn't allow me to crack open an Easter egg and not think twice about the chocolate bunny. I ached from the top of my mouth to my toes. Like somebody was kicking one of my teeth with a steel boot. They dragged me in the rain to Mercy. Said they couldn't do nothing for me cause today was Easter Sunday. Not even an aspirin. No authority. My gum was pounding like drills breaking new cement and I couldn't think. Maybe I was supposed to be too young to think. I cussed at the nurse. Called her a stupid white bitch. They refused to help me get rid of the pain. My mama had to call the dentist at home, interrupting his duck and glaze. He was not upset. He understood pain, stopped it. But was not into preventing it. He prescribed a pill strong enough to dull an elephant's keenest senses. Not mercy. No mercy was there. The next day he did not give me enough Novocain to deaden the pain and he knew it. Instead of saving the tooth, he yanked it out and threw it in the trash. There is a blank space there now, he could have prevented this.

Is he okay, will he be alright. Can he talk.

Yes, his mouth is twisted and he sounds funny, but he makes good sense. He's watching the World Series and smiling. He knows what happened to him and doesn't like it. Says he's inconvenienced, can't move his right arm too good. May not be able to plant his garden come spring. Pick his grapes and pound them for wine. That bothers him. If he could just lose a little weight, bending over might not be so bad, he says. People are so nice to you when you get sick, he says. He likes this attention, but would prefer to be at home. Says he has a color TV that works better than this one right here at Mercy. Can't turn it up too loud, wake up the intensive cares.

Confrontation

When I first met him, he was real nice. Still is. But I decided, this time, to be honest. Just tell the truth about everything. So when he asked me first off what sign I was, I told him a lie. Then he said "humph." Started making his own calculations and assumptions. Then he asked me where I came from, so I told him, "Nowhere," I just got here. Then I spit out the truth, quite bluntly:

"First of all, I'm thirty years old and got two college degrees. I'm a writer and attractive and get hit on like this all the time and ain't found a man yet who could keep me interested for more than two years and one who could handle all this I got at once and still feel like a man himself and that's what I'm looking for. Scared yet?" His eyes hung out of the sockets.

"Do go on," he said, "I'm entertained and need to be enlightened."

"Now, if you want pussy, speak up, cause I got it and it's good. If you want to be platonic friends, which usually means we fuck every now and then, let me see more of you first before I decide if it's worth the effort. If you simply want plain old pussy, let me think and look even further into this before I decide if you're worthy of a slick trick and some fast ass and I'll gladly give it up if you're half as good as me. But, if you're seriously looking for a woman, not an imitation or a perpetrator, but a friend, a dedicated trick, a companion, a lover, mashed together, someone to understand you and someone you can talk to who will be willing to take the time if you're willing to take the time, then, buddy, you've found yourself a thoroughbred woman. No shags, no tags, pure woman."

When I looked up I was sitting in the room alone. The door was cracked and the small breeze that flowed in tickled my chin. I smiled to myself in the mirror, tears tearing up my stomach.

I wish men were easier to find, if not rescue.

Don't, Vernita

I always knew something was wrong with that man. Anybody that grin as much as he do, is up to something. Ain't never seen him mad, in the ten years since I been living right next to em. He trims them hedges, whistling. Eyes like the devil's, I always seen it in em. Couldn't fool me. And Vivian. She about as dense as they come. I been press and curling her hair off and on for 'bout seven years, till here lately, she stopped asking me to do it. Don't look to me like she been washing it neither. Something is wrong with her. He done done something to that woman, them kids, over there, and I betcha I know what it is. I always seen that sneaky grin on his face, just like my ex-husband's, and it told me right off not to trust him. Of course I been friendly as can be all these years, but I ain't no fool. A person ain't guilty until he do something, even if you know they thoughts ain't no good. And he sits up in church every Sunday, right in the front, like he ain't never sinned. But I knowed a snake when I see one, and this one been crawling places he ain't had no business. Tell me I'm lying.

Today I Got a Letter

I plopped down in my free-with-miles first-class seat on Air France, happy to finally be able to get away from everything and everybody. A divorce can weigh you down and make it hard to get back up. But I climbed.

"Would you like a cocktail or a snack before we take off?" the pretty flight attendant asked. His makeup was perfect. Under different circumstances I would've asked if he would share his tips with me or take me upstairs and give me a makeover. I'd be willing to pay a week's salary to look alive and galvanized. Freedom is expensive.

"Thanks but no thanks," I said.

"Vacationing in Paris?"

"Celebrating," I said without catching myself.

"What are you celebrating?"

"My divorce."

He holds up his hand to give me a high five.

"I have felt your pain. But freedom feels good, doesn't it?"

I hadn't thought of it this way, but I suppose I was legally free but I was waiting for emotional freedom. Twenty-two years is a long time. Especially since it meant marriage had taken up half of my life. And I was bored with him for one-third of it. But it turned out I was not alone.

I don't speak French because there was no reason for me to learn it. I used to speak Spanish in college. Which came in handy in Southern California. It was also my minor. Sociology was my major. What a waste. And then I made the biggest mistake of all and went to law school.

"Would you like me to put your carry-on up top for you?"

"No, but thanks."

"So, how long will you be in Paris?"

"A week. Long enough to figure out what to do with my future."

"It's a good place to start. But I'll bet you know already."

I looked up at him. Sincerity pierced through his blue contacts. Which was when I closed my eyes.

I reached down and pulled out about six envelopes, all bills, except for one, which looked like something I hadn't seen in years: a letter, handwritten, addressed to me, from a Mona Witherspoon. I had a cousin whose name was Mona but her last name was Diggins. Like mine once was.

I dropped the bills back inside my carry-on and squeezed the envelope. It was so thick it bulged, so much so that she had put Scotch tape on both sides of the flap to seal it. I hadn't seen this in years. When I wrote my college boyfriend and enclosed pictures of myself although he never wrote me back. He preferred using collect calls, which I had to pay out of my student loan money. Until he stopped calling altogether. I was fickle as hell back then. And maybe I never evolved.

I didn't unseal the envelope because if it was bad news I didn't want to hear about it at thirty thousand feet.

Three Zeroes

"How much longer do I have to wait?" Myrtle asked the young Asian receptionist. She was at her latest attorney's office. She'd been calling him ever since she left Cecil's this morning but because he had not returned her calls for two days she'd decided to just take the Metro to Arcadia. Even if she had a car and even if she knew how to drive Myrtle still wouldn't have driven because the 210 was always backed up.

She was pissed. Fuming. Fanning herself with her Lakers cap and tapping her right foot at about fifty rpm. Something had told her not to get a Chinese attorney this time. They were too damn honest. She was of a mind that this claim would've been done quick and in a hurry. It's not like she was asking the store for all that much. Four grand wouldn't break them. This was just enough to compensate for her pain and suffering and enough to pay her rent for four or five months since she'd been on disability almost two. Myrtle regretted taking that overnight bus trip to Vegas and losing that little chump change Baskin-Robbins had paid her when she slipped on a melting ice cream cone after she saw that little girl drop it.

She had to catch up.

Myrtle had also gotten bored sitting around waiting for this settlement on top of missing work because her sciatic nerve in her right buttock did hurt when she sat down too fast or had to reach too far for something or when she bent over to pick up something. She couldn't help it if she was clumsy and was always dropping stuff. Which was why to relax, sometimes Myrtle took a Xanax to be able to enjoy sex. But even then she often got complaints because she didn't move all that much and Myrtle insisted on being on the bottom because bouncing up and down was out of the question. Just to make sure she crossed the finish line first, she often relied on her hands or her mouth to finish him off. But Myrtle was at the point now where sex was more of an inconvenience than it was worth. She had ordered a little gadget off the Internet but the batteries ran out too fast and usually at the wrong time. She had learned from experience that remembering her favorite orgasms was almost as satisfying as having them.

"Miss Leatherwood?" the receptionist finally said, waking Myrtle up. She'd forgotten where the hell she was. She picked her baseball cap up from the floor and fluffed her short hair, thinking it was time for a perm.

"Yes," Myrtle said, about to jump up from her chair but catching herself by the time she'd reached about six inches, and then limping over to the desk. For a minute she had forgotten she wasn't in the doctor's office.

"I'm afraid Mr. Lim won't be able to fit you in this afternoon. He's due in court in an hour and since you didn't have an appointment . . ."

"Why won't he return my calls?"

"He sent you a copy of the letter he received from the insurance company."

"When? What did it say? How long will the settlement take?"

"Well, after reviewing your X-rays, their insurance company had a hard time seeing any injuries to substantiate the pain you've been complaining about."

"So they think I've been faking being hurt? Is that what you're telling me?"

"They have denied your claim."

"What the fuck did you just say?"

"Please don't use that kind of language, Ms. Leatherwood."

"I'm sorry. But I thought Mr. Lim was a much better lawyer like his ad claimed. I won't be recommending him, that's for damn sure. Have a good day."

And then she romped over to the door and slammed it shut.

By the time the elevator finally got there, Myrtle's head was throbbing and her ears were ringing and all she could hear was the sound of the ATM card popping back out when she asked for forty dollars and the screen said her account was overdrawn. The other machine Myrtle heard was the slot machine telling her she had lost again.

She knew she should've gone to the Black lawyer she'd seen on TV but her injury was only chump change and probably wouldn't pay for those commercials so they wouldn't take her case. She'd tried a few others but they'd all done a little research and discovered just how many personal injury claims Myrtle had filed in the past four years: seven.

Myrtle had assumed she would walk away with at least five or six grand, especially since she really had slipped and fallen this time. Someone had knocked a bottle of Palmolive dishwashing liquid off the shelf and while reaching for Dawn (which she preferred over Palmolive because Dawn cut grease better) she didn't see the small green puddle until the heel of her right brown Ugg had slid through it and she fell on her behind. Myrtle looked around to see if anybody could help her but what she was really hoping for were witnesses, preferably an employee, but no one was in the aisle except her. She also could've screamed out but she didn't. Instead she pushed her six-foot, two-hundred-pound self up to a standing position and realized that this little fall wasn't worth complaining about. Until a few days later when she started getting spasms in her neck.

She went to a doctor. They did an X-ray. It was not serious. The doctor suggested she ice it and gave her a prescription for an anti-inflammatory, a muscle relaxer, and a non-narcotic pain pill she favored over the other medications. She decided on her own to get the neck brace mostly because she liked the attention.

"What happened to you, baby?"

"Did you break your neck?"

"Do you have to turn your whole body to see something on your right or your left?"

"I hope you're suing them."

Yvonne, of course, was on to her.

After Myrtle left the attorney's office she was thinking maybe this was bad karma for all the other times she exaggerated her injuries—lied when she got right down to it—but on the other hand she also felt like what was the point of having insurance if you didn't use it? And most of the businesses she sued should be more mindful of the shit in their aisles or on their shelves and on the floor—stuff people could get hurt from.

Now, this no-settlement meant she was going to have to go back to work. The last thing Myrtle wanted to do. She was so tired of working at Hummingbird Gardens she didn't know what to do. Tired of smelling and bathing and touching and turning over old people and especially taking them to the bathroom. She did her best not to let them know this. It wasn't their fault they couldn't do any of these things for themselves anymore. But some of these old motherfuckers were mean and nasty and liked to swear at her and pull on her uniform. Myrtle assumed one day she'd probably end up in one of these facilities and she hoped somebody would be kind to her even though Myrtle knew she was probably going to be just as much of a bitch at eighty as she was at forty-six.

She did not like this line of work but it was the best she could do considering she had bypassed college because Myrtle knew she was not college material and since she had no secret talents and no marketable skills she was aware of, when her cousin Sally asked if she wanted to work here, Myrtle felt any job was better than no job. This was almost ten years ago. Sally went on to nursing school. Worked at UCLA Medical. Myrtle wished she'd been smart growing up but she prided herself on being well-informed because everything she felt she needed to know was on BET.

Myrtle truly believed there was nothing else she could learn how to do this late in life that would allow her to live like a normal person. All she wanted to do was be able to pay her bills on time, have a little left over for a weekend in Vegas, and maybe visit her relatives up in Oakland and the handful she heard were still alive in Durham, North Carolina. Good thing she never had kids. Good thing she'd only been married once but he got killed in a car accident after six months of marriage and Myrtle was afraid to say I do again. Not that she'd been asked. In fact, she hadn't even been in love since then. She had friends she could call to fill in the empty spaces. Sometimes, they called her. This worked. They went home or she went home. Nothing lost.

Being an only child is what Myrtle thought made her feel so lonely. She didn't know how to confide in people. Didn't know how much to tell and how much to keep to herself. Yvonne, though, had a warm ear. Myrtle liked her. And even though Yvonne never gave up much personal information about herself, Myrtle envied her because she could tell Yvonne was happily married and plus she was the manager of a high-class restaurant. Yvonne was always teasing her about her most recent accident, but Myrtle had to tell somebody the truth and Yvonne didn't seem to judge her. It was the reason Myrtle ate breakfast there at least three or four days a week. Hell, it was cheaper to eat at Cecil's than going to the grocery store and buying all the stuff. And who could be bothered? She even had a tab. In fact, she owed Cecil's sixty-seven dollars, which she knew Yvonne kept track of in that little orange notebook in her uniform pocket. But Yvonne never said anything to her until she was getting close to a hundred.

She decided to walk the six blocks from the Metro to her tiny one-bedroom garden apartment with no garden. She did not know how to decorate and didn't much care. She liked IKEA but didn't trust the furniture they sold because it was too pretty to be so cheap. Except for those paper lights she favored and she loved their napkins and glasses and cups and especially those big blue bags she used to take her dirty clothes down the hall to do her laundry. All the furniture in here was used but comfortable.

She sat down at the tiny glass kitchen table and looked around. Her life was boring. There was no zest to it.

"This is your fault, Myrtle," she said aloud, and then reached inside her black purse and took one of those painkillers and swallowed it without even thinking about getting a glass of water. She was wondering if maybe she should get a pet. One that didn't make any noise. Something she wouldn't have to walk. Not a bird because they tweet. And not a cat because she couldn't stand the sound of that purring. Maybe some fish. But she'd have to clean the tank. And plus they die. She shook her head no for even thinking about pets.

Myrtle then looked over at her slot machine. It was almost real. It paid quarters. She bought it on eBay four years ago after she broke her foot and couldn't get up the bottom step on the gambling bus. Myrtle had come to the conclusion that she might have a small gambling problem but it wasn't worth going to Gamblers Anonymous over.

When she heard Etta James singing "At Last" coming from her cellphone she knew it was her mother. But Myrtle was not in the mood to hear anything her mother had to say. She always wanted something Myrtle didn't have to spare: money. In fact, Myrtle wasn't all that crazy about her mother because she lied about things she didn't need to lie about. And could not be trusted. Jane was an old version of Bonnie without Clyde. Myrtle decided to microwave a bottle of iced coffee and took a few sips until she felt the painkiller melting and entering her bloodstream, which provided her with the tolerance she needed to listen to her mother's voice message: "I know you're listening, Myrtle, but I just want to know if you would be willing to go to church with me next Sunday. I'm thinking about joining."

The last time Myrtle went to church with her mother she had a twenty-two-caliber pistol in her purse. So no, she was not going. Myrtle hit delete. She would call back before Sunday and pretend to have a sore throat.

When her stomach growled Myrtle knew she was hungry but did not feel like cooking and her refrigerator was empty and she did not feel like going to Cecil's twice in one day and plus she did not like their dinner dishes. It's pretty hard to fuck up breakfast, she thought, which was why she started her day there since it was within walking distance of work. Speaking of which.

She picked up her cellphone and called her job. She hadn't been in in over a month. She knew Miss Alabama of 1970 would answer and sure enough she did. "Well, if it ain't Miss Pasadena of 1980! When are you bringing your butt back in here? You know Ruth and Little Miss Sunshine are missing you something fierce, but the bad news is Henrietta has gone to glory, so what can I do for you? And please don't tell me you're still suffering from yet another unsolved injury, Miss Myrtle."

"Hi, Cathy Anne. I'm sorry to hear about Henrietta and I

wish I could say I miss Miss Ruth and Herlaine but I don't, but I'll be back in next week as soon as I get cleared with HR. And I'll have you know I've had real muscle spasms in my lower back but thanks to physical therapy and deep-tissue massages and very little medication, I'm like a good used car."

"Good good good. And I don't believe you don't miss the Girls. You try too hard to be a hard-ass. Just wait until you're old and wrinkled and can't walk or remember shit, you'll pray someone puts you in a place like Hummingbird Gardens, where you can get business-class care and don't have to worry about being abused. Anyway, Henrietta left all of us a little something."

"What did you just say?"

"I said Henrietta left all of us a little something."

"Can you spend it?"

"Hell yeah. I was able to pay quite a few car notes, get some of my credit cards down to a zero balance, which will help my FICO score go up, thank you, Jesus, but of course everybody's rewards were different based on how fond Henrietta was of you. I know some folks have exaggerated their versions of the truth because Henrietta wasn't crazy about too many folks and you and I both know she was not fond of Black people. But hell, a gift is a gift is a gift."

"She sure squeezed the hell out of my free hand whenever I fed her, and the glaze in her eyes was warm, so maybe some of my Blackness rubbed off on her. Anyway, this was awful thoughtful of her. She was one of my favorites."

"No she wasn't. She cursed like a sailor. She was a bitch. Even her kids knew it. We all knew it."

"Regardless, I appreciate whatever she was kind enough to give me."

"You are so full of shit, Myrtle. Anyway, the envelope is in your cubby."

"Would you mind opening it for me, Cathy Anne?"

"Yes, I would mind. It's supposed to be personal, which also means private, so you either have to wait until you clock in or stop by, which would just be tacky if you ask me since you haven't been here for over a month."

"Damn you, Cathy Anne."

"Don't tell me you're hard up for cash?"

Myrtle didn't want to tell the truth, so she didn't. "No, but who couldn't use a few extra dollars?"

"Then just wait. If I hadn't told you, you wouldn't have even known. I should've kept my big mouth shut."

"You know that's impossible. Bye. See you next week."

Truth be told, Myrtle really didn't care how much it was although she was praying it had at least three zeroes behind the first digit.

Walk-By

Now that Buster was free, he didn't know where to go. He had only stopped by Cecil's because he was hungry and afraid his brother wouldn't have any decent food available for him to eat. After he'd gotten off the bus, he was surprised the diner was still there. It used to be Wetzel's. And it used to be pale yellow but now it was a dirty blue and looked like they'd added about ten coats of paint over the years. Inside hadn't changed much except the floor tiles were too gray and the counter was too fancy. Swirled fake marble. Buster was just hoping the food was still good. It was, which was why he started out with the basics: eggs, bacon, potatoes, and cinnamon toast. That Yvonne lady was a little short with him at first, but Buster knew it was because he probably sounded ignorant, was asking too many questions he should've known the answers to, and was getting on her nerves. But she softened up, which was why he had already decided to go back once he got settled.

He was also grateful to his one and only brother for letting him stay with him, even though Chester never visited him in all those years. Buster really didn't know why, and didn't ask. Not seeing each other after all those years was like being in that *Back to the Future* movie. They were young when he left and now they were both certified old. No sense holding a grudge for not acting brotherly. For not accepting any more collect phone calls after the first six months. For not sending more than that two-hundred-dollar money order that Buster had given Chester his

PIN number to take out of his savings account, which Buster knew had a balance of a little over three thousand dollars because he had been saving up for a house for him and his wife. No, the past was where it belonged. The blanks should just stay blank. They would just go from here.

They had spent the first few days trying to catch up. But Buster knew you couldn't possibly catch up after more than twenty years. As they sat there eating a Hungry Man meat loaf dinner, Buster watched what he had learned was called channel surfing, but Chester suddenly grabbed the remote and turned the television off.

"I just finished going through my midlife crisis," he said for no reason Buster could think of.

"Well, I missed mine," Buster said.

"Stay as long as you need to," Chester said.

But Buster already knew he wasn't going to be able to live with his brother. Chester wasn't tidy. And there was an odor Buster didn't appreciate. The plaid sofa they were sitting on dipped in the middle and the colors all blended into one, which was what Buster called ugly. The wooden tables were splintered from the bottom of beer bottles sweating and none of his dishes matched. Even the rug was so thin it moved when he walked across it. Chester didn't seem to realize how poorly he was living and Buster didn't feel he was in any position to tell him or complain.

He also had no idea who his brother really was, didn't know what kind of man he had turned out to be, but by the looks of his house—which Buster knew qualified as a teardown—it didn't seem like Chester—who was sixty-nine, four years older than him—had taken advantage of his freedom to do more with his life. Chester claimed he was forced to retire early from a job he had not bothered to acknowledge and said he'd been on social security disability for a number of years although Buster hadn't been able to figure out what his disability was. It looked like loneliness.

By the end of the first week Buster had summoned up some courage and walked outside but didn't go past the sidewalk. He was trying to get used to the idea of freedom, and plus he didn't know where to go. Couldn't remember who he had forgotten. Time had erased a lot.

That evening, Chester brought home a bucket of KFC for dinner. They were sitting on the couch again. *Headline News* was on.

"Hey, brother, ain't they supposed to be compensating you for being wrongly accused?" Chester asked. "I saw it on a CNN special a while back."

"They're supposed to. One hundred dollars a day for every day I was locked up," he said.

"How much is that?"

"About six hundred ninety-three thousand."

"Goddamn. That sounds like a whole lotta money but not for all the years you lost. How soon can you get it?"

"I don't know, man. It's a slow process."

"You don't have no idea?"

"Could be months. Could be years."

"Well, what you supposed to do in the meantime?"

"I don't know."

"Hell, I forgot what you was doing before you went in. What was it again?"

"It's not important. I can't do it now anyway."

"Hold on now. You worked for HUD. As a housing inspector. I remember," he said, proud that he had. "Hey, they took this shit off your record, right?"

Buster nodded.

"They have to."

"It can take time, too. And they ain't in no hurry."

By the end of the second week Buster went outside and stood in the front yard. He was tired of being in the dark. The house next door blocked the light coming into his room. It also felt like a lot of people had slept in his bed, which was why Buster decided to walk the eight blocks to Target and bought a set of light blue clearance sheets and a bundle of light blue towels and he also discovered Febreze.

Of course Buster didn't have a driver's license and wasn't even sure if he remembered how to drive, which was why when Chester reached out to hand him the keys to his fifteen-year-old Corolla after telling him, "Some things you never forget," Buster disagreed and dropped the keys on the concrete driveway like they were hot. He didn't trust himself behind the wheel. It would mean he'd have to be responsible for the lives of others. He would have to pay attention to red green and yellow lights and left and right blinkers and these thoughts made him jumpy.

"Where you trying to go?" Chester asked.

"I don't really know," Buster said, lying. But he decided he wanted to see the house they grew up in but he didn't want his brother to come with him.

"Well, good luck," Chester said, and went on back inside his raggedy little house.

Now Buster sat close to the back row on the nearly empty bus. Pasadena had sure changed. It was more colorful. Taller, newer buildings had taken over Colorado Boulevard and he was thinking that maybe he would even go to the Rose Parade this year. Sell something. Or, just watch like he did growing up. He liked the horses. The Clydesdales, mostly. Because they were bigger and stronger and yet graceful, like the women he always preferred.

Altadena touched Pasadena. They were like first cousins. The San Gabriel Mountains were like green wallpaper that lined the sky except sometimes—like they were today—the peaks were capped with snow even though it was eighty degrees here on the ground. Buster looked out the window like a tourist just to remind himself he was free. There was nobody in particular he wanted to see, which was why he had decided to go see the house he had grown up in. It wouldn't ask him any questions, and it might be good to remember where he came from and to see how the neighborhood had changed. Plus, he could say hello and goodbye to his mama and daddy, both of whom had passed while he was locked up. Buster was going to have to ask his brother where they were buried, and just hoped he remembered.

He wondered if the house was still stucco. He knew it had probably gone through many colors and there would be no flecks of the mint green peeking through the top layer. Paint was the new skin. He wondered if the grass he used to cut was cut in a different pattern than the crisscross way his daddy had showed him to make it special. If it was neon green. If the avocado tree was full of dark brown pears.

When he felt tears rolling down his cheeks he covered his eyes because he was not on the bus. He was back in his cell. Wondering, how long would it take for those people from the Innocence Project to read his letter? He knew they received thousands and he had no idea what number he was. He stopped counting the years after the first four or five and then didn't care how long a year was. He just waited. For the end to get there so he could start a new beginning.

And then it came.

He had been exonerated.

He liked that word.

All charges dropped.

Twenty years stolen.

There were no apologies.

It was like being let out of a cage.

That's how long it took the State of California to realize he did not rob anybody. He still wondered what DNA stood for. What took them so long to discover it? And why didn't they test everybody accused of crimes to make sure they didn't have to depend on just eyewitnesses?

More than half the men he lived with in prison claimed they were innocent. He knew who the bullshitters were. He knew who was really guilty. And he knew who wasn't. But they all got treated like criminals. Like slaves. They had no power. No rights. Just tiny "privileges."

He had no idea how to start over. In fact, he couldn't even remember where he'd left off.

He had not fathered any children that he was aware of.

Bernice, the woman he had been married to for two years, divorced him after he'd been there less than a year. He understood.

When the bus stopped close to the street he grew up on, Buster knew the walk would be an inclining one, but he had just purchased a pair of black and silver Nikes in an attempt to make them also double as dress shoes. When he stepped off the bus the sidewalk was so hot it looked like thousands of diamonds were growing up from it. He could see the heat.

He needed water.

A Subway was on the corner so he walked over and went inside. It was so cold he wanted to sit and drink his water before heading back up the hill, which was why he'd bought two bottles. He drank the first one in one long gulp. Then began to walk up the street he'd lived on for sixteen years of his childhood. He wasn't sure why he was doing this. What he was expecting to find. Feel. Or, see. What good would those memories be? Really. He remembered the word nostalgia. He had looked it up in the dictionary when he'd read it in some book. He was not home-sick. He just wanted to see if he could measure the length and weight of his life since then. He was maybe hoping he could see his future in the front yard.

But the house was gone.

There were five floors of condominiums looking down at him. Gray and yellow. There was a small patch of grass that did not need to be cut; a trimmer would do the trick. The sidewalk was now gray. Cobalt-blue planters on both sides with some kind of tall succulents reaching for the sun. The evergreen was still there. Tall and strong. He looked up at where he assumed his bedroom window once was. It was a patio.

"Excuse me, sir," a young white woman in jogging shorts pushing a stroller with twins said to Buster. "Just trying to get the babies home!"

Buster backed away and moved to the left so she could pass. He didn't wonder when their house might have been torn down. In fact, there was construction up and down this long street. He decided he had seen enough of what was gone. And just kept walking. He didn't know where he was going: which corner to turn. He was trying to get used to being free and when he saw a park he had forgotten about, he walked up the steps and saw it now had a big blue band shell on the far side. Buster sat down on a bench, rested the palms of his hands on both knees, and pre-tended an orchestra was playing.

ESSAYS, SPEECHES, & OPINIONS

"Looking for Mr. Right" is from the February 1990 issue of *Essence* magazine and touches upon a sensitive subject: the successful late-thirties Black female's inability to find a mate or to have an enduring relationship.

Looking for Mr. Right

[1990]

Maybe it's just me, but I'm finding it harder and harder to meet men. And when I do, the atmosphere often feels strained, as if they're thinking, "She's probably another woman over thirty looking for a husband." They're right.

Times sure have changed. When I was in my twenties, I don't remember it being all that hard to meet a man and get familiar, even though we may have ended up only being friends. But these days, if you're "serious," men look at your interest in them as entrapment. They don't like being "pursued" and as a result tend to back away. Lately my girlfriends and I, who are all over thirty, are spending more time looking for or trying to develop some kind of strategy that will result in landing a lifetime companion. What it boils down to is a guessing game: How should we act? What should we say or do that won't seem threatening? It's sad to think that we've gotten to this—that we actually have to think about how to go about finding a man. But what's even sadder is that some men make you feel guilty for looking. I don't feel guilty.

I grew up and became what my mama prayed out loud I'd become: educated, strong, smart, independent, and reliable. "I don't want you growing up having to depend on no man for everything," she always said. But she didn't suggest for a minute that upon gaining a certain kind of professional recognition I'd not need or want one. Now it seems as if carving a place for myself in the world is backfiring.

Never in a million years would I have dreamed that I'd be thirty-eight years old and still single. I am not embarrassed about it, just tired of it. I had planned on being married by the time I was twenty-four, but instead I went to graduate school. Ended up loving and living with a number of men who, for whatever reasons, didn't take life as seriously as I did. At thirty-two I had a baby, and not long afterward I split from my son's father.

I haven't had a steady man in my life for so long that I'm beginning to wonder if I'll ever find one. I spend more time thinking about sex than actually doing it, and sex was something I never imagined I'd have to get used to doing without. I keep asking myself, what am I doing wrong? I've done what I consider to be all the "right things": I still look good, I'm honest, and I have a lot to offer someone. So why over the last few years have I had only two powerful but short-lived relationships, in which both men just stopped calling one day with no explanation? "They're probably just scared," my friends said. Scared of what?

Sometimes I think that even though a lot of "professional" men claim to want a smart, independent woman, they're kidding themselves. Some of them seem to feel secure only as long as you're passive, don't take much initiative, and let them call the shots. But as soon as they realize you're not willing to sit in the backseat because you also know how to drive, they feel so threatened they try to figure out ways to get you to back down, back off, or just acquiesce until you appear to be tamed. I'm not tamable.

In the good old days, men seemed more aggressive. They would walk up to you in a minute, strike up a conversation, ask you for your phone number, and then follow it up. I can't count the times recently when I've walked into a social gathering where there were plenty of men, but for some reason they either didn't acknowledge me at all, or if on a lucky day I happened to be noticed and contact was made, there was this businesslike quality in their voices, as if I were a prospective client. The warmth is missing.

I remember when folks used to have house parties—not brunches—on Saturday nights, when all you had to do was call up someone and ask where the party was and you went, and other folks came and brought their friends, and we all talked and laughed and danced. Lots of times you spotted him or he spotted you, and he probably asked you to dance, and if you felt something special being in his arms or liked the tone of his voice or what he had to say after the song was over, then the night became much too short. There was a genuine, organic level of excitement and curiosity that has been replaced by a slew of superficialities: what you do for a living; how much you make; how you dress; if you'll make pretty babies. I miss the casual intimacy we used to have.

The other day I was driving with all the windows rolled down, blasting Anita Baker and Tracy Chapman back-to-back, and I became grief-stricken. Every time I hear their songs, I end up remembering the men I've loved, how good it was then, and just how empty my life often feels without a man in it now. I turned off the music because I got sick of feeling sorry for myself, and then I wondered, just when did things start to change? By the time I pressed the garage-door opener and pulled inside, it was clear: I didn't have these problems when my life didn't have any real definition, when I wasn't making much money, when I hadn't published much of anything.

Last summer, an ex of mine said with some glee, "It's lonely at the top, isn't it, baby?" Although I'm certainly not at the "top," as he put it, I got his point. It is lonely "out here." But I wouldn't for a minute give up all that I've earned just to have a man. I just wish it were easier to meet men and get to know them.

Just last night, as I sat on the top step of this big beautiful house I bought in the desert and looked out at the mountains, the phone rang. It was my mama. "You sitting at home again?" she asked. I didn't feel like explaining how tired I was of going out just in hopes of meeting someone and how it always failed. I'm tired of the search and want someone to find me. I hung up and heard a woman on the radio singing something about "I thought we'd be happy ever after." I cried a little and then cried some more. I felt entitled. Then "Keep On Movin'" played. I felt a boost. I looked at all the space I have in my house and started laughing out loud. Hell, maybe I'll throw a party, invite all my friends from all over the country, get some of those blue lights, and play some Smokey or Aretha or the O'Jays, and maybe, just maybe, I'll even spike the punch.

Submitted to *The New York Times* as an op-ed in response to the beating of Rodney King and the subsequent acquittal of the responsible LAPD officers, "This Is America" is raw, indicting, and representative of the pain many people, especially Black people, felt in the immediate aftermath of that verdict. While McMillan reflects on this particularly explosive period in 1992, she also lays bare arguments that continue to echo across America more than thirty years later. This piece is from McMillan's personal collection and is being published for the first time here.

This Is America

[1992]

The focus is on our anger, not the injustice.

I remember when I first saw that videotape. I wanted to hide my face but I couldn't. I thought for sure it was shot in South Africa or Afghanistan, but no, the newscaster said Los Angeles. And it was 1991. The cops were kicking Rodney King like he was a dog who'd bitten them, beating him with their billy clubs as he lay curled up on the pavement. They clubbed him sixty-seven times.

In the following weeks, I, like millions of others, watched the tape over and over, feeling more enraged each time. "They'll go to jail," is what my friends and I kept saying. "It's an open-and-shut case. It's in living color." The evidence of police brutality was indisputable; we were certain that for once the police would be held accountable. Guilt for them would finally be inescapable. Hah!

When the verdict was handed down on Wednesday, I was at a barbecue across the street from where I live in the Bay Area. I had forgotten to bring the sweet potato pie I had made. I ran home to get it and, after a seismologist had gone on and on about earthquakes and aftershocks and faults, I saw the television announcement that a jury in Simi Valley, a mostly white suburb of Los Angeles, had acquitted the four police officers on all counts, with the exception of one officer who'd be tried for one count of assault. Then the screen cut to the beginning of riots in South Central Los Angeles. I felt ill.

I mean, twenty years ago I lived in Los Angeles, when it was a clean, safe, relatively boring place. And then I remembered when the police started flying over homes in South Central Los Angeles in those helicopters, and how it seemed as if overnight L.A. had become a police state, at least where Blacks and Hispanics lived. You never saw a helicopter fly over Beverly Hills or Malibu.

It breaks my heart to know that President Bush thinks America is still such a great place for everybody. It angers me when I'm told to put my hand over my chest to say the Pledge of Allegiance, to sing "God Bless America," when I see this kind of flagrant racism and am asked to accept it.

I'm mad. Everybody should be mad. How did this trial ever manage to take place before a jury with no Blacks? And, despite this, why were the jurors unable to see right from wrong? Don't white folks believe in God? Don't they believe in justice? After all, they're the ones who created the Constitution, the Bill of Rights.

The jury based its verdict on what Rodney King purportedly did before the eighty-one-second video was shot. What could one man do to four men armed with guns and clubs that would merit this kind of violence?

Watching the fires burning on TV, I understood immediately why people resort to violence. When you feel helpless and angry and there's nowhere to turn for help, you strike out at anybody. Mayor Bradley can't do anything but beg, and no one's interested in listening to him. I'm not.

I lived in Arizona for three years and hated it because not only could we not get Dr. Martin Luther King's birthday made into a holiday, but the white folks were happy about their power, over how they had not let it become a holiday—they felt triumphant.

In my mind, there's no greater crime than overt injustice. This one was in color. When four officers go free, when Mike Tyson goes to prison and William Kennedy Smith doesn't, when Clarence Thomas is appointed to the Supreme Court to make a point about justice, I am reminded that America remains a racist and perverse place to live.

And when you are fortunate to live in a pretty neighborhood, pay your bills on time, and write books that people read, people think you can be shielded from the harsh realities of this nature. Well, I'm not that shielded. And millions in this country aren't either.

My brother is in prison right now. He was arrested ten miles from Simi Valley for drunk driving. Fortunately, he didn't get beaten. How many white men have gone to jail for the same offense? How many innocent Black men who have been beaten never made it on videotape? And now, what difference would it make?

I have never trusted policemen, even the smiling ones. That badge stands for more badgering than safety, and the power it confers has forever gone to some of their heads. When you give men power, they usually abuse it, and this incident is no exception.

The humiliation and outrage that Americans—whites and Blacks, people of color alike—feel is valid. We're entitled to it, and now the focus is on our anger and not on the injustice itself.

This is America. The land of the free. Home of the brave. Well, I'm not buying into it today. I do not believe in violence, but if we have to do what we did in Watts in 1965 to let the Los Angeles Police Department, the city, and the government know that we're not going to tolerate this kind of travesty, then I say we have to make our point any way we can.

I really don't want to see innocent people hurt; already too many have died, many more Black than white. As African Americans, we don't have that much time as it is and when we burn and kill, it's usually in our own backyard. I hope we don't do that.

It's unfortunate that this case, as an acquittal, can never be appealed. I wonder how Rodney King is feeling. I wonder if the jurors would feel differently if he had been their son.

My brother should be back at work. Those jurors should be forced to know what it feels like to be kicked and hit with a baton while lying on concrete. And those policemen should've been behind bars a long time ago. Praying for guidance. Something. A conscience maybe.

"An Icon, but Not a Hero" was published in 1994 in the *New York Times* opinion section. In a world that insists on viewing things as black and white, McMillan gives us a more nuanced response to the double murder trial of O. J. Simpson.

An Icon, but Not a Hero

[1994]

O. J. Simpson has been a hero to millions, but he wasn't one of mine. I thought of him as a great athlete who was handsome, articulate, had a charismatic smile, and could run through airports to get a rental car faster than anybody I knew. But hero?

My heroes are more vital than that: Nelson Mandela. Jesse Jackson. Randall Robinson. Malcolm X. Jean-Bertrand Aristide. Dr. Martin Luther King, Jr. Ben Chavis. Arthur Ashe. To name a few. Men who've stuck their necks out for their beliefs.

O.J. has been more of an idealized figure, carved by the media. Poor Black boy from the ghetto overcomes the odds, becomes a football star, movie star, a purported gentleman. White folks loved him because he played by their rules and epitomized their ideal of the All-American Black Male.

Even so, as I watched the evidence mount against him, I kept my fingers crossed that he hadn't done it—that someone who hated him had set him up, that some other wild scenario would emerge, showing that he wasn't capable of brutally murdering his wife. We'd already been embarrassed by the Mike Tyson thing.

The Michael Jackson thing. Rappers being busted left and right. Now here's another Black man falling from grace. The perfect media target.

But he is not the foremost role model for young Black boys. A lot of kids have never heard of O.J. Besides, they have new sports heroes. Magic. Shaq. Michael Jordan. Barkley. Sure, O.J. was held in high regard, but I seriously doubt ten-to-fifteen-year-old boys' hopes and dreams will be shattered because one athlete suddenly plummeted from stardom to hell. As far as I'm concerned, athletes corner too much of the media market as it is.

My guess is that Hollywood has already called Denzel to find out his schedule. If they hurried, this could be a made-for-TV movie and be on in time for the fall sweeps. Maybe Dominick Dunne has already hopped on the red-eye and is digging up the dirt on O.J., Nicole, and Ronald. They're likely to have already changed the cover of *Vanity Fair* the way they did when Jackie O died. This is even better than the boring Menendez boys.

O.J. is the kind of man Black mothers wanted their daughters to grow up and marry. He married a Black woman (whom he supposedly never hit) and left her for a wealthy young blond beauty queen who never had to work a day in her life. But he also beat his white wife.

A relative told me: "Well, to be honest, I never liked him. That's what he gets for marrying that white girl." As if this entire spectacle was payback, his punishment for crossing that racial line. Many Black women resent Black men who marry white women, in part because so many unattached, successful, desirable, educated Black women are having a tough time finding a desirable, educated, successful, unattached Black man. Some of us are jealous. Feel that we deserve the O.J. types more, particularly since too many of our men are in prison, unemployed, or drug abusers.

I grew up watching my mother run to the kitchen to get butcher knives and skillets to keep my father off of her. Men don't just hit you once. They always swear it'll never happen again. My father thought he owned my mother. Couldn't stand the thought that she refused to be his possession. She lived in fear. Did everything in her power so as not to set him off, provoke him. He wanted her world to revolve around him. But it didn't. And she got tired. Tired of being scared. Tired of wearing a leash. Long after she divorced him, she looked over her shoulder, until he remarried and left her alone.

It's not merely a "family matter," as O.J. put it. It's deeper than that. When women are physically abused and nothing is done to stop the battering, the woman often ends up killing the man or he kills her.

O.J. worked very hard to live up to his image, but whatever his demons were, they eventually won out. They said he'd been depressed. Despondent. Having a hard time coping. With what?

Maybe O.J. simply snapped. It took a long time for it to happen, and now innocent lives are lost and a tragedy has become a circus. Two children have lost their mother. And what if it turns out that this megastar-superhero did kill her? How are they going to live with that?

Plenty of folks, white and Black, are secretly enjoying the spectacle of a successful Black man's fall. I'm not one of them. (And yet the double standard of treating celebrities differently from the average Joe Blow also infuriates me.) O.J. is simply one fallen Black angel. We have plenty of others. I'll be glad when reporters and cameramen give true Black heroes one-tenth of O.J.'s airtime for their acts of courage instead of waiting for their wings to break.

This short piece is from the anthology *Dick for a Day,* edited by Fiona Giles, published in 1997. McMillan's signature pull-no-punches style offers a glimpse of how she would approach the world as well as her curiosity about what men have and what they do with it.

Dick for a Day

[1997]

First of all, I'd want to have a big one—and I'd show everybody.

I think there are two ways I could look at it. If I had a penis, sexually speaking, I would have the ultimate sexual experience with a woman. I would surrender myself and ask her to tell me whatever it is that she really wants me to do, and I'd do it. But if I had a penis just for the sake of it, I would like to see what it's like to be a man, to feel his adrenaline and get inside his head, just to see what a man feels and thinks throughout the course of a day. I would like to see if having a penis really makes all that much difference.

An alumna of UC Berkeley, McMillan addressed the University of California, Berkeley, class of 1999, twenty years after her own graduation.

UC Berkeley Class of 1999 Commencement Address

[1999]

First of all, I want to say congratulations and way to go to each of you graduating seniors. I can't remember if I graduated from here in 1977 or '78. What I do remember was there was some kind of issue with my not passing a Spanish class or something, but since I'd already been accepted into Columbia University's MFA film program, I think someone here told me tough noogies. But I also think I begged and pleaded to take anything except Spanish 5 because I had trouble conjugating my verbs: I hated preterites and subjunctives (who needed them). They were confusing for me and would I ever really need to know, considering the fact that I was clairvoyant and knew that one day I would simply be able to log on the Internet and write anything in English and hit the translate button and wham! Every verb conjugated for me! I got lucky. They let me take Cultural Anthropology. I think I passed that.

Anyway, what I do remember quite accurately is being accepted to attend this university. I was in shock, because although I was a good student, I was no genius, as I'm sure most of you are. All I knew was that I wanted to save the world any way I could, and I had heard that this was a good place to learn how to do it. Back then, Berkeley was on the quarter system, which was a totally new experience for me. I thought I was hallucinating when after my first week I realized I had thirteen books to read in like nine weeks or something. I was thinking, do they offer an Evelyn Wood speed reading class here or what? I mean, just to name a few, and I still remember the color of these books: We're talking John Kenneth Galbraith, *Don Quixote, One Hundred Years of Solitude, A Treatise of Human Nature, Their Eyes Were Watching God,* and then there were the essays for comp class that got on my nerves and we can't forget Spanish.

Needless to say, I was overwhelmed, but when I looked around, nobody else seemed to be freaking out, and I was not about to be a casualty my first quarter here. So this is the place where I can honestly say I learned how to read. I learned how to listen. I learned how to write and how to voice my opinions. This is the place where I realized that your opinions mattered. Maybe only to my friends, but it was more than I was used to.

As an aside, this might be a good time to throw in a few more enlightening experiences I discovered. That would be marijuana: Hated it! But did that stop me? Nope. All my friends did it, so I kept my stash under my sofa in a shoebox top for my friends but because of that one time I smoked too much and actually died one night on my waterbed, I started faking it: pretended to inhale, and since they were all buzzed they never even knew the difference.

Okay. Let's fast-forward the film a couple of years? I got the biggest surprise of my life: I could not save the world by myself. The world was much bigger than I thought. We mortals had an ocean of problems on an individual and not just global level, that seemed like a good place to start. Of course I—like everybody else who happened not to be some prodigy—was totally confused when at the onset of my junior year my counselor asked me a ridiculous question for which I had no concrete answer: What major are you going to declare?

How the hell was I supposed to know? At any rate, during this same time period, I had developed this hobby called writing. I also had developed another habit which I still have: running my mouth, speaking up and out when I think there has been some wrongdoing, so I started writing these scathing editorials for the campus newspapers and a lot of bad poetry which publications desperate to fill up blank pages would actually publish and then I took a fiction writing class from Ishmael Reed who told me I could write and I knew he probably told all of his students this bogus line so I didn't believe him but I would show my little stories and poems to my mama, who was almost but not quite impressed because her big question was: Can you make a living writing this mess?

Well, who'da thought? That lying and exaggerating and even manufacturing the truth and writing more mess would one day be how I actually made my living and that this mess would also enable me to buy her a home and a new Lexus and then there was that cruise to the islands and those new sets of dentures? Who'da guessed it?

Not me.

I didn't listen to my mama. She meant well. Because she wanted her oldest daughter to amount to something. She wanted everybody back home in Michigan to be proud of the first McMillan to attend and graduate from college, but she also kept her fingers crossed that I would get a real job and make some real money. After all, isn't that why people go to college?

That never really crossed my mind when I got here, to be honest. I wanted to get an education. I wanted to be smarter. I wanted to learn everything I could about everything I could. I was nosey and curious and fascinated about the world and people and the role we could play in it once we gained all this damn knowledge. The idea alone of being fortunate enough to have an opportunity like this excited the hell out of me. I wasn't worrying about how I was going to make a living. I was only twenty-one years old! That was all I was supposed to be thinking about? How I was going to make a killing after my little stint here? I knew lots of students who were obsessed about the idea and a lot of them seemed to know which income bracket they were striving or destined for. I never really thought about it, not in those terms, because back then, and even now, how much money does it take to make you happy or qualify you as being a success? I don't know.

What I was more concerned with was finding out where I was supposed to fit. If I was going to have to carve out a way or stumble on it. In retrospect, it's easy to see now that I had already found it but was too young or stupid or naïve to know it. Writing was a hobby. I took it seriously but I did it mostly because it made me feel good, it offered me an opportunity to get things off my chest, and later, helped me develop two things I lacked most and wanted to feel more: compassion and empathy. I didn't understand then and still don't know what makes us as human beings kill each other, hurt and abuse each other, break each other's heart, betray someone, and why do we lie? Why do we always have to come in first? What's wrong with a bronze medal if it's your best? Why do we need a million dollars to be happy and if you get it, does it matter if you have to step on someone else's toes or knock them out of the way to get it? What would make two middle-class boys go into a high school and open fire? How does it feel to be an Albanian right now? I have never been evicted before—I take that back, I have—but how does it really feel to be run out of your country with children and no money and no food? I can't even begin to imagine.

My mother died when she was fifty-nine years old at my house while I was in Rome. I was on my way out of the hotel room to buy her a pair of shoes I'd seen the evening before when I got a phone call with a voice on the end I did not recognize and it was from a doctor and when I hung up the phone all I knew was that I had to go home and make arrangements to bury my mother. That was what I thought he said. But that was impossible, because last night I'd called her and she told me I had been invited to the White House by President Clinton and she begged me to go even though I already had other plans. I promised her I would. I asked her what was she doing opening my mail and she said it said the White House on it so she thought it was important. She could not believe that her daughter had been invited to the White House by the president of the United States. I remember joking, and telling her that if I had taken that job at Channel Two News like she had hoped I would, did she think I'd be going. She told me to shut up and find something nice to wear.

Who'da thought?

Which is why I want to assure each and every one of you today that if you aren't sure what you want to do with the rest of your life, it's okay. Don't freak out. Don't worry if your parents are nervous and wondering if their money is going to go down the drain if you decide to be a ski bum for a year or two or travel around the world or work at Kinko's until you can figure a few things out. It really is okay. Tell them to take a chill pill.

Your twenties are probably going to be the most confusing time of your life. I think it's one of the best times of your life. You are being tested. To see what you're made of. To see how resilient you are. If you've got the right stuff. Your world won't be over if you stray off the path and do a few destructive things. Oh, I forgot: I left out a few things, or I should say years. There was like this four-year stretch of time after graduation that I sort of became a few drinks shy of being an alcoholic and a few lines short of being an Ivy League cokehead, but of course my mother didn't know this. At the time, I didn't know how scared I was about my life, that I had yet to find my place, but it wasn't until I realized that I was headed in the wrong direction, that I was a college graduate and on the verge of becoming a drunk and a drug addict, that I snapped out of it and decided that so what if I was confused: Hell, almost everybody I knew was, but what I also knew was that drugs and alcohol didn't exactly clear things up for me.

So, I stopped. And when I did, I started writing. Clearly. And then things did start clearing up for me. I wasn't numb anymore. I realized I had feelings that I could transfer to fictional characters and try to make some sense out of them. I realized that I was not alone.

All this is to say once again that after you leave here today, if it takes you another few years to get it together, take it. If you're on your way to law school or med school or rushing out to get that MBA because Mom or Dad wants you to, you better pay attention to what's screaming inside your own head. Pay attention to it. Don't listen to your parents' fantasies about what they want you to do. They had their time and they did what they wanted to do. Now it's your turn. I say pay attention to whatever you feel truly passionate about. It may not be in Boalt Hall or IBM or, heaven forbid, Hollywood!

I feel sorry for a lot of you guys, because the pressure to succeed and compete is so intense now, who the hell can even enjoy college anymore? The stress on my fifteen-year-old is unbeliev-able and he's only in ninth grade. I've complained to the teachers that kids do not need four hours of homework a night. They need some downtime, to be kids. And the same is true on the college level to some extent. You guys have been students, but in some ways, you've been prepped to be superhuman. It used to be a 4.0 was a coup. Not anymore. I never knew you could get a 4.3. And even that's not good enough to get you into Harvard or MIT. You now have to have a long list of community service performance on your résumé, and being class president wouldn't hurt and didn't you have time for any sports? I think it's ridicu-lous the pressure that you guys are and have been under and you should give yourself a big round of applause for being here today. Because you deserve it.

Personally, I suggest a vacation. Anywhere. Do something really stupid. Something that makes absolutely no sense. Be irrespon-sible for a minute or two and hang loose because I truly believe that what they say is true: You are only young once. Enjoy it. This is the one time in your life where you can afford to make mistakes. It's the one time in your life where you can change your mind and the world will not come to an end. It's better to go ahead and be a beach bum in your twenties than in your for-ties. I think it sounds tempting, but know that life is an accumu-lation of experiences, and how you handle those experiences has a lot to do with the quality of your life. That success has more to do with being happy because you're doing what you want to do with your life, not what you think you should be doing. It doesn't matter if you don't become a millionaire. It shouldn't matter if you are never famous. I never aspired to be on the *New York Times* bestseller list or to make millions of dollars from a book. The money's not bad, but it was not my goal. I wanted people to read my books so that they would feel better about themselves but it has taken a lot for me to feel good about myself. I wanted respect. I wanted my stories to make people feel valid. To give them strength, and perhaps courage. And that, to me, is worth far more than fame and money. And that is what I believe in my heart I learned at this institution. The only regret I have is that I think I slept through my commencement, and I do not recall ever actually receiving my diploma so if there's anyone here with any connections, I would certainly appreciate seeing my name in a different kind of print. Just for nostalgic purposes, you know. Thanks a lot for having me, good luck to each and every one of you, and don't forget to stick your neck out, take as many chances as it takes, and when you think you're there, I hope you know that you aren't, that the beauty of this process is that it's an ongoing one. I say, strive to be a good person, a compassionate person, a confident and able one. Give something to the world instead of seeing what the world has to offer you. You won't be disappointed. I can almost guarantee it.

In October 2016, McMillan looked back and offered life lessons in *Real Simple* magazine from her perspective as a Black woman in America who, despite the opportunities, accolades, and success, still has to fear for her son in a world that is still learning that Black lives matter.

Life Lessons

[2016]

On March 3, 1991, I watched the breaking news in horror as Rodney King lay face down on the ground being repeatedly kicked and beaten with nightsticks by four white police officers. It happened in the very same Los Angeles suburb where my sister and her family lived. All this for speeding? It was surreal, but for weeks, millions of us watched this video over and over and over, trying to understand why these police officers were doing this to this young man. They, of course, did not know they were being videotaped.

FAST-FORWARD.

On April 29, 1992, I was at a barbecue across the street from where I lived in the Bay Area and had forgotten to bring the sweet potato pie I had made. I ran home to get it and saw the television announcement that a jury had acquitted the four police officers. Then the screen cut to the beginning of the riots in South Central Los Angeles. I stood there, paralyzed, and when my neighbor—who happened to be white—knocked on my door wondering what was keeping me, I pointed, then handed him the pie and told him I wasn't hungry. He canceled the barbecue because, like me, he was shocked and pissed that these police officers were not going to be punished for committing a crime that was clearly motivated by race.

FAST-FORWARD.

When Barack Obama was elected president, I thought it said a lot about how far we'd come as a country. However, the night of his inauguration, I heard rumors that more than fifteen Republican congressmen and strategists had met at a D.C. restaurant and conjured up a plot to block every piece of legislation President Obama presented to them. I thought it was just gossip. But eight years later they have demeaned and insulted him and made false claims about his birth—even his religion. They've done everything except call him a nigger in public.

FAST-FORWARD.

We still have a race problem in America, and the body count is rising by the day: Tamir. Laquan. Freddie. Philando. Eric. Rumain. Ezell. John. Akai. Tony. Walter. Philip. But these aren't all of them, not least because this list doesn't include women. And yet the Black men who murdered police officers in Dallas and Baton Rouge were killed on the spot.

I have a thirty-two-year-old son, a Stanford University graduate. I raised him in an upper-middle-class neighborhood in the Bay Area. Many of his friends were white, Asian, Mexican, Black, and Muslim. None of them made much of it because they were buddies. But he's tall, muscular, and dark-skinned, and he's been stopped by police officers for no apparent reason. He knows what not to do or say, but it apparently doesn't matter.

A few years ago, my son showed me a photo of himself standing in a boat holding a large fish in the middle of a lake three hours outside of Memphis, where he lived at the time. I asked if he'd gone with a friend, and he said no. "Are you crazy?" I said. "Do you realize you could get stopped and killed on those highways for no reason whatsoever, and I wouldn't even know where you were?" I was in tears. He apologized and promised he wouldn't do it again. I didn't believe him.

I want to know how police can justify shooting a Black man for selling loose cigarettes or CDs—or a child all alone in a park playing with a toy. Or why people would be pulled over because they have a broken taillight or a wide nose or are dark-skinned, like my son, just because police think he fits the description of a suspect. And how can you force a woman who hasn't done anything to the ground, forcefully arrest her, and then shrug it off when she later dies in custody? I'm at a point now that if I had car trouble and a police officer stopped to help me, I'd be afraid to roll down my window.

FAST-FORWARD.

In 2013, the Supreme Court struck down the heart of the Voting Rights Act after forty-eight years, giving states the right to rig the voting requirements in a way that was racist and ageist. I was apoplectic. My ex-boyfriend's mother, who is eighty-three, doesn't know where her birth certificate is, doesn't read very well, no longer drives, and doesn't Uber. I promised to take her to her polling place. "I was able to vote for President Obama," she said, and still has her little ticket to prove it.

But a lot has changed in eight years. Now we are in the midst of the scariest, most bizarre election for president I've seen since I came of voting age in 1969, making it even clearer just how racially divided this country still is.

My neighbor, who happens to be white, doesn't understand why so many white people believe that too many African Americans and Hispanics have stolen their jobs. Her family emigrated from Ireland. I tell her how shocked I am that so many white people have stereotyped us by believing we're lazy and don't even belong in this country.

I would like to remind them that we weren't exactly invited here; we didn't come willingly, and the fact that some white people resent us for taking advantage of the opportunities offered to every American is beyond my ability to comprehend. When I watch the news these days, the vitriolic tone of some of the rhetoric feels like we're heading back to the sixties and seventies. I'm not going. My son recently called to say, "Mom, did you know there are twenty-one women in the world that run countries?" I told him I did.

But this is America.

I just want us to respect each other for the content of our character and not be disrespected because of the color of our skin. We are Americans. And as the late Rodney King said twenty-five years ago, "Can't we all just get along?"

BIBLIOGRAPHY

Published Fiction

McMillan, Terry. "The End." *Yardbird Reader* 5 (1976): 284–92.

McMillan, Terry. "Touching." *Coydog Review* 2 (1985): 75–83.

McMillan, Terry. "Reconstruction." *River Styx* 20 (Spring 1986): 61–72.

McMillan, Terry. "Ma'Dear (for Estelle Ragsdale)." *Callaloo* 30 (Winter 1987): 71–78.

McMillan, Terry. "Quilting on the Rebound." In *Voices Louder Than Words, Volume 2: A Second Collection,* edited by William Shore. New York: Vintage, 1991: 29–45.

McMillan, Terry. "From Behind the Counter." In *The 1619 Project,* edited by Nikole Hannah-Jones, Caitlin Roper, Ilena Silverman, and Jake Silverstein. New York: One World, 2021: 329–32.

Essays, Speeches, & Opinions

McMillan, Terry. "Looking for Mr. Right." *Essence,* February 1990.

McMillan, Terry. "This Is America." 1992. From the author's personal collection.

McMillan, Terry. "An Icon, but Not a Hero." *The New York Times,* June 25, 1994.

McMillan, Terry. "Terry McMillan." In *Dick for a Day,* edited by Fiona Giles. New York: Villard, 1997: 14.

McMillan, Terry. "UC Berkeley Class of 1999 Commencement Address." May 11, 1999.

McMillan, Terry. "Life Lessons." *Real Simple,* October 2016.

All unpublished pieces are from the author's personal collection.

ACKNOWLEDGMENTS

Working with Terry, I've worn a number of hats, and the labor and love required to bring these early and little-known works out of the file storage has been the most rewarding.

Any book is a miracle. The circuitous journey of this collection started with Lucy Carson's mad document-scanning skills. The archives team at the San Francisco Public Library, the microfiche room at the University of California, Berkeley, and the Harlem Writers Guild provided invaluable assistance. Thank you to Ishmael Reed for hearing Terry's voice when you did and for lending your inspiration to this volume.

Abundant gratitude for Crystal McMillan's inspiring focus and patience, Hilary Teeman's intuition and expertise, and Molly Friedrich's support looking back on more than forty years as Terry's agent.

Deepest love and thanks to my home team: my daughter Xoxa, my mom, and Amy, Chandra, Ella, Kai, Leon, Liz, Liza, Rachel, Tioni, Yvonne, and my family around the world.

Thank you to Terry for twenty-five fun years of adventures in creativity, collaboration, and dreams come true. Your trust in me to do your early work justice has meant the world.

Finally, thanks to Virginia Dunwell, Terry's friend and early reader since her days as a student at UC Berkeley, for keeping track of the letters, early drafts, and newspaper articles while she moved from Hawaii to the Hudson River Valley and locations in between. Your friendship and faith in Terry never wavered. We wouldn't know a fraction of what we do without your archive.

PERMISSIONS

ABOUT THE AUTHOR

TERRY MCMILLAN was born and raised in Port Huron, Michigan, and discovered her love of literature while shelving books at the local library. She burst onto the literary scene in 1987 with her wildly acclaimed *New York Times* bestseller *Mama*, which won the Doubleday New Voices in Fiction award in 1986 and an American Book Award from the Before Columbus Foundation in 1987. McMillan's signature humor, wisdom, and warmth made *Disappearing Acts, Waiting to Exhale, How Stella Got Her Groove Back, A Day Late and A Dollar Short, The Interruption of Everything, Getting to Happy, Who Asked You?, I Almost Forgot About You,* and *It's Not All Downhill from Here* all *New York Times* bestsellers. *Waiting to Exhale* and *How Stella Got Her Groove Back* were made into award-winning major motion pictures that proved huge at the box office, and *Disappearing Acts* and *A Day Late and a Dollar Short* were adapted into successful made-for-TV movies. She was also the editor of *Breaking Ice: An Anthology of Contemporary African-American Fiction*. She was awarded an Essence Lifetime Achievement Award in 2008. Beloved by her fans, McMillan's books have sold millions of copies worldwide.

terrymcmillan.com
Instagram: @therealterrymcmillan
X: @MsTerryMcMillan

ABOUT THE TYPE

This book was set in Bembo, a typeface based on an old-style Roman face that was used for Cardinal Pietro Bembo's tract *De Aetna* in 1495. Bembo was cut by Francesco Griffo (1450–1518) in the early sixteenth century for Italian Renaissance printer and publisher Aldus Manutius (1449–1515). The Lanston Monotype Company of Philadelphia brought the well-proportioned letterforms of Bembo to the United States in the 1930s.